Allan E. Ansorge

Crossing the Centerline

Echelon Press
Publishing

CROSSING THE CENTERLINE
An Echelon Press Book

First Echelon Press paperback printing / July 2009

All rights Reserved.
Copyright © 2009 by Allan Ansorge

Cover Art © Nathalie Moore
Award winning Graphic Artist

Echelon Press
9735 Country Meadows Lane 1-D
Laurel, MD 20723
www.echelonpress.com

All rights reserved. No part of this book may be used or reproduced in any manner whatsoever without written permission, except in the case of brief quotations embodied in critical articles and reviews. For information address Echelon Press.

ISBN: 978-1-59080-635-7
1-59080-636-0
eBook 0-634-4

PRINTED IN THE UNITED STATES OF AMERICA

10 9 8 7 6 5 4 3 2 1

For:
Tony, Laurel, and Chris,
who all pretend I never falter,
and mostly for Jane who never does.

A thank you goes to those who protected and served: Mike Porter, Mark Smith, and Pat Mitchell.

A special thanks to Stefanie Lazer, the voice of reason in what I write.

A big thanks also goes to my sister, Linda, who listened to the book, three pages at a time, long distance, and is still casting the movie in her mind.

Thank you, Jane, for showing me every day that dreams can come true.

CHAPTER ONE
Things That Go Click In the Night

It wasn't what Detective Michael McCaffery heard that woke him, but rather what he didn't. Something familiar was gone. He had been living on the boat *One Fine Day* for three weeks now. The groans of the lines, the squeaks of the dock bumpers, and thumps of the hull had given him many sleepless nights. By now he was used to all he should have been hearing and wasn't.

He lay in the queen-size bunk in the aft cabin and tried to figure out what had changed. Mike really didn't want to brave the dew before the sun was high enough to drive the chill from the air. There was something wrong, though; he could feel it.

Mike was a transplant from New York's Hell's Kitchen, a true Irish Copper. He claimed to be what his grandfather called Black Irish, which prompted most people to think he was Italian. Whatever his inherited traits were, they did not include a love of the sea. He never cared much for water of any sort, especially if it wasn't in a glass and couldn't be called a chaser. But when a friend asks you to keep an eye on the one thing left in this world that he truly loves, you compromise.

For the last month, someone had been vandalizing boats in marinas up and down the Wisconsin, Lake Michigan shoreline from Port Washington to Kenosha. The timing couldn't have been worse for Mike's friend Carl to leave his boat unattended for a month.

Carl had enrolled in a Coast Guard Auxiliary course in Florida, studying for his captain's license. He hoped to start a new career on the water. His last job, as Mike's partner on third shift as a sheriff's deputy, ended abruptly a year and a half ago. A stolen semi-tractor demolished his car, his right leg, and the lady he planned to marry.

Carl was, after all, Mike's oldest and best friend, depending on how you measure them. He knew Carl would risk his life for him–and had. You don't say no to a guy like that, even if it was to babysit his dumb-ass boat for a month or more.

Mike dragged himself from the bunk and crossed the cabin floor with an ear tuned for anything unusual. There was nothing at first; then the boat moved with the wake from an early morning charter boat going out. Instead of hearing the air squish out of the big white bumpers between the boat and the dock, Mike heard *click*.

Now where did that come from? Had he left something loose on the deck?

"This damn thing better not be sinking," Mike yelled as he bumped his head on the companionway hatch for what seemed like the five-hundredth time. "Damn small doorway," he cursed. Mike never considered that maybe through the years–all forty of them–he'd grown a shade wider and perhaps a bit less agile. In the cockpit, he bent over, swearing under his breath. While he held the top of his head with both hands, he felt through the thick black curls for seeping blood.

"Son of a bitch! Damn, damn, damn!"

Click.

There was nothing loose on the deck. Mike waited for what seemed to be a damp, cold forever, then *click*. It was behind him; no, beside him. It seemed to be coming from the boat itself. It was louder out here than below. It had to be close.

Mike stroked one last tender touch at the growing lump on his head. Quietly, he stepped off the boat to the edge of the dock and waited. Another boat passed, the wake hit…*click*.

The click came from the rear of the boat. Carl always backed the boat into the marina slip. He called it the Mediterranean style of tying up. When Mike moved toward the stern, he found the source of the noise was plain to see. Tangled in one of the lines was a denim-covered leg. Mike presumed the rest of the body was below the water line. A buckle on the side of the boot at the end of the entangled leg tapped the hull once again. The leg's only movement was caused by the waves of the lake. Mike's years of experience in law enforcement left no doubt in his mind: this leg was dead.

Train well and the game is easy… Unlike detectives on TV, a real detective calls the cops even if he is one himself. Mike dove into the cabin, clearing the head-bruising hatch by at least a quarter of an inch. He started the search for his always-misplaced cell phone. Finding it really didn't matter; as usual, the battery was as cold as the water around the body outside.

Exiting the cabin didn't go as well as entering. Skull Bump Number Two was well into development as Mike entered the bait shop at the end of the pier. Dialing the sheriff's office on the pay phone, Mike appeared to be the only one not to notice he was wearing a baggy pair of boxers and nothing else.

Because the dispatcher recognized Mike's voice, the call for an ambulance and investigating team took but a few seconds. By the time he got back to the boat, everyone within a city block seemed to be standing between him and suitable apparel. He had to get some clothes on before all his peers showed or he would never hear the end of it.

Fortunately, no one else went in the water trying to catch a glimpse of the leg. Some even voiced their disappointment at how little there was to see.

Mike had dressed before the rescue squad arrived. He also managed to produce a pot of coffee for the people he normally worked with, who now crowded the dock.

Gallows humor flowed about in an effort to ease the tension officers always felt when dealing with death. No one wants to be near death, even those who train and get paid to endure it.

"So, Mike, is this some angry husband who found out, or just someone you owed money to? Ha-ha...." came from somewhere in the group. Mike ignored it.

He knew he was going to have to call Carl and it wasn't going to be nice. Carl would realize, of course, it wasn't his fault, but he was pretty particular about his boat. Someone dying on it wasn't going to go over well, Mike could sense it.

Suddenly the word *liability* popped into Mike's head. He started looking around to see if there was something he had done to contribute to the demise of Old Dead Leg over there. Although he wasn't a religious person he heard himself say, more as an expression than a prayer, "Oh God, don't let someone sue old Carl. I don't think he could take a shot like that right now. He was just getting his shit back together, please just leave him alone."

The shift commander touched his arm. "Were you talking to me, Mike?"

"No, Cap, I was just thinking out loud."

Just then, the firemen making up the rescue squad lifted the body up onto the pier and the medical examiner moved in. Time seemed to drag on forever; Mike felt the sun touch his face.

Everyone did his or her job in turn. After the medical examiner came forensics, then the detectives. Not that there was a lot for them to do. The first thing they found in their effort to identify the body was an overabundance of identification. The only thing worse than no ID, in the process of putting a name with a body, is finding too much. The body carried five driver's licenses with five different names on them.

They all knew then this wasn't going to be a simple case of drowning. A body that cannot be positively identified automatically becomes a John Doe–in this case five John Does. Everyone on the pier knew the average vandal doesn't bother to create five different identities for himself.

CHAPTER TWO
Now You See It...

The first cell-phone-to-cell-phone call from Mike to Carl was less than successful. Carl was on the Gulf of Mexico, ten miles west of Sanibel Island; Mike was negotiating traffic on I-94.

The best Carl could make out was Mike took a ride on the boat, or he took someone down on the boat. Neither of the two was very likely. When Mike started to say something about "five niceties," Carl gave up and decided to call him back later to see what it was all about.

Carl never made the call. As he thought it over, he concluded there was little or nothing he could do for Mike for the next three days anyway. He was just two exams away from his precious license, what seemed to him to be a rebirth of sorts. He would be home in two and a half days. Whatever Mike did or was doing could be dealt with then. After all, how bad could it be?

Mike never tried to call again. The news, he discovered after the first call, wasn't the type of information he thought Carl should hear over the phone.

After recovering the body from the lake, the wheels of justice ground on. Two detectives from a district other than Mike's were assigned to the John Does, all five of them. This was normal procedure when an officer was directly involved in a mysterious death. Mike's boss told him he thought it would be a good idea for him to take a few days off, just until things got straightened out.

In spite of all of Mike's unsolicited advice, Detectives David Miller and John O'Connor had not yet been able to put a name to the body. All five of the driver's licenses had been obtained, somehow, for people who had passed away at least two years ago. John Doe, or perhaps someone else, had gone to a lot of trouble to make certain it wouldn't be easy to determine exactly who he was.

After coming up empty on the licenses, Miller and O'Connor caught a break. They–or rather the computer–found a match for one of the fingerprints taken from John Doe. His right thumbprint was a near perfect match for a partial one on file that was found on the fuel cap of a stolen semi-tractor involved in a hit-and-run over a year ago.

Mike believed in the occasional coincidence, but stupid he wasn't. He didn't need a building to fall on him. This wasn't even close to an accidental drowning of a boat vandal; this guy had been hunting Carl.

Mike's mind went back to the accident scene. He'd always thought there was something strange about it, but he could never put his finger on it. He should have read the accident examiner's report at the time, but it had *seemed* like an accident. It took him less than two minutes after he left Miller and O'Connor to get to the lower level where the Case File Room was located.

Mike loved the file room. It was quiet, and the

only other person there most of the time was a police aide he'd had a crush on for the last six months. In one and the same room, a beautiful girl and piles of paper Mike viewed as a treasure trove of promotional opportunities. It just didn't get any better than that. He had spent hours here even before personnel had hired Bernadette to replace the evil-tempered, hairy old man who had been born to complain constantly.

Mike always felt if he spent enough time scouring the ceiling-high racks of files, one day he would find the one unsolved case he would crack. The brass ring would be his and the promotions would rain down on him like manna from Heaven.

Bernadette believed it too. She also believed in Mike just enough. So she set aside any case files she came across that might get him the splash he would need to make his ambitious plan come true.

Officers weren't authorized to enter the caged file area, but the wannabe deputy, with shoulder-length brown hair and eyes to die for, was more than willing to find the files on the hit-and-run.

Bernadette was gone from view for about fifteen minutes, which certainly wasn't up to her normal efficiency. When she came back to the gate, she was empty-handed.

"Sorry, Mike, it's not there. I'm certain it should be in section A-31, but it's not. Let me check the log to see if someone has it out."

"Tell me, were either Miller or O'Connor in here this morning since, say, nine o'clock?"

"No, you're the first person in today since I opened the doors at seven."

Crossing the Centerline

"Would you please check the log to see who checked the file out last?"

Bernadette gave her computer mouse a smack to activate the screen and plopped into the desk chair. This was a chance for her to impress this Mike guy; instead, she was coming off looking like an idiot. He was cute in a stumbling sort of way, polite compared to all the jamokes who tried to hit on her or the ones who made rude comments about how she filled out her uniform. He was nice. She really hoped one day, instead of asking for endless files, he would ask her out of this paper dungeon.

The screen lit up; within seconds, her rapid keystrokes told her, and she told Mike, the file was never checked out. Therefore, officially, it had never moved from A-31 since it entered the cage over a year ago.

"I don't think you have to look for it any more, Bernadette."

"Maybe it was just misplaced. I could start a manual search for it, Mike."

"Don't bother. That file was assigned location A-31 the day it came here, right? If the file was never checked out but isn't here, I think someone has taken it with the intention of it never being seen again. Don't worry about it. I'll take care of it." After a quick goodbye to the woman he hoped would become the love of his life, Mike headed outside into the fresh air to think about what he had learned.

The right thing, he guessed, was to call Miller and O'Connor and put the picture together for them. He was sure they would never tie Carl into this before he got back. Although he barely knew the detectives assigned to the case, they didn't strike him as balls of fire, or even like they made up a decent candle flame between them.

Oh boy. He had better call Carl to tell him to get his ass back here. As Mike began to dial Carl's cell, he thought better of it and snapped the phone shut. If someone was still trying to kill Carl, as of now he or she obviously didn't know where Carl was and that was a good thing.

Mike drove back to the marina. He climbed over the yellow tape that had been strung around the boat earlier that morning to protect any evidence there.

There was nothing more to be learned here and Mike knew it. The man with no identity, or rather five of them, wouldn't have left a trace if he hadn't worn leather-soled shoes on a slippery deck–something any boat savvy person would have known.

Mike also figured if the guy had tried to kill Carl twice in eighteen months, he probably wasn't in this alone. Persistence of that kind is usually bought and paid for. Mike could only surmise that someone would try again. Well, Carl was safe where he was…for the time being. The thought occurred to Mike that perhaps he should try to hide the boat for a while so it couldn't be tampered with.

How would one hide a boat that big? It's not like you can drop a camouflage net over the thing. Mike would have to move it, but to where? Only two people would know where Carl took it for repairs; but it would be ideal to surround it somewhere else with more boats. Mike had no idea where Carl would take his boat to get it fixed. As much as he loathed the thought, he dialed Carl's mother.

He didn't dislike Maggie; quite the contrary. She was everything someone who should have been a grandmother by now could be: slightly on the plump side, with snow white hair done at a salon every Thursday. She had all the social graces, but also the vocabulary of a drill sergeant when she wanted to leave someone dazed and shaking in their boots.

The downside to Maggie was she was damn nosy. She had the ability to keep you talking just long enough. Before you were aware of what was going on, she knew everything inside your head and then some.

Unlike some of her peers, Maggie not only kept pace with the times, but, for all intents and purposes, she was towing the rest of her world behind her. She had become so computer savvy she started her own website to guide some of her less adept cronies through the weird world of hardware and software. This had upset some of the younger peddlers of similar services because she got free ad space in senior magazines due to her age.

About two months ago, Maggie sold her home and lied her way into an assisted living center because they offered free broadband. The food in the optional dining room wasn't half bad. The deal closer was if she ate there full time she might never have to wash a dish again. Maggie had perfected her phony arthritic limp to such a degree Mike and Carl often forgot she never had the affliction.

It's said the Irish can talk the birds from the trees,

but Mike knew he was no match for Maggie. Getting the information he needed without telling her someone had tried to kill her son, and may try again, wasn't going to be easy.

"Michael! How nice of you to call. How are you? We have to talk fast, dear. I have an online karate class in ten minutes. How is life at sea, or at least at dock?"

"Funny you should mention the boat," Mike said, plunging straight into the fray, then pausing for just a moment to ponder online karate lessons. "I was wondering where Carl took his boat for repairs, you know, that place with the big shed they put them in." He was grasping at straws now.

"Michael, have you broken Carl's boat?"

"No, no, nothing like that." It was a small island of truth for Mike to stand on while he caught his breath. Sweat started to form on his forehead. "I know they sell a lot of nautical stuff at those places. I thought I would get the new captain one of those hats with the gold braids."

The silence on the other end of the line crushed down on Mike to the point where he was ready to break down and tell Maggie all. She finally broke the standoff.

"You're not good at lying, Mike; don't get into the habit. You obviously know something you feel you can't tell me. I can respect that, but I will eventually find out what it is if I have to beat it out of you. The address is where it always was, in the black book under the radio; look under Repairs."

Without a goodbye the connection went dead.

Boy, is she pissed. Distracted by how stupid he had been not to search the boat before he had called Maggie, Mike again attempted to remove the companionway hatch with his head and achieved a new record for really foul language.

After the twelfth ring, a voice lower and slower than a southern senator on Valium answered, "Meyer Boat Works."

Still holding his head, Mike asked how long it would be before they could stop by to pick up a boat he needed stored for a couple of days.

The voice came back like it was prerecorded. "Don't store boats here, we fix them, and we got all of those we can handle right now. Besides, we don't pick up or deliver neither, thanks for calling."

"No, wait, it needs some work, all right. I want you to make that door you climb through to get downstairs bigger. I bump my head on it a lot."

"How long you had a boat, fella?"

"Well, it's not really mine; it belongs to my friend, Carl Fletcher. I thought I'd get it fixed for him while he's out of town."

"I know Carl. Does he know you're about to cut holes in his boat?"

"Oh yeah, it was all his idea. He's real big on this."

"Tell you what, fella, you bring her over as soon as you get topside–I mean upstairs–and we'll work out a price, but we'll wait till Carl stops by to give us the go ahead."

Mike could hear a rumble of laughter as the line went dead. He wondered what that clown thought was so funny.

The location of the keys was nearly all Mike knew about running the boat. Desperate men make desperate moves, so he headed down the pier toward Benny's Bait Shop again. He hoped by now they had forgotten his last appearance there in his underwear.

Some type of buzzer sounded as he sauntered into Benny's, this time fully clothed and displaying his most congenial smile. "Benny around?"

"Not hardly. Benny's been dead for nearly fifteen years," snorted a redheaded teen from behind the cash register. He gave the appearance he hadn't combed his hair for two days, and his attempt at a goatee was failing miserably. His voice was about two octaves higher and cracked a lot but came through with the same slow drawl as the man who'd answered the phone at Meyer's. Mike wondered if there was a lot of inbreeding in the Bay Harbour boating community.

"I need someone to drive a boat over to Meyer's as soon as possible. Do you have any idea where I could get someone?"

"You could get me, if you've got the money to pay me. It would be about fifty bucks in advance. I close here for a while every afternoon."

Mike winced twice, but felt he didn't have much of a choice. "Deal. When can we go?"

Within minutes they were ripping yellow police tape off the boat. Teddy, the self-christened captain, had his hand out for the cash as they floated free of the dock. When he gave both of the engines full throttle, Mike was thrown on his back in the cockpit.

Crossing the Centerline

At the rate they were traveling, it took Teddy less than three minutes to clear the end of the dock and another three to slam them nearly full tilt into the dock at Meyer's.

As Mike struggled to pick himself up from the floor of the cockpit, he heard a familiar voice. "Damn you, Teddy, you nearly wrecked my dock again. Does your old man know you're driving a boat? He ain't fixed the hole you put in his yet."

Teddy tossed the keys to Meyer and, with fifty dollars in his hand, headed for the horizon at a dead run.

While Meyer, as his friends called him, tied up the boat, he laughed as Mike retrieved his weapon from under a deck chair.

Mike gathered himself and asked, "Since it was just next door, why didn't you come get the damn boat?"

"Liability and lawsuits, son. It's making cowards of us all. Now, you and I both know Carl don't want no holes in this here boat; we both know you've been living on her while Carl is down south; Carl told me you would. We both know some chucklehead died trying to climb aboard her in the middle of the night. So what gives?"

"I don't know for sure myself," said Mike as he showed Meyer his police ID. "I just don't want anything to happen to Carl or his boat until he and I can figure it out."

"Carl is a good man," said Meyer, "and you're a good partner just like he said. The boat is invisible until you or he says otherwise."

CHAPTER THREE
Coming Home

Mike wasn't afraid of Carl; they had known each other far too long for that. All the same, he was nervous as he waited for Carl's arrival at the baggage pickup at Mitchell International Airport. Carl was supposed to be on a flight with a posted 10:35 am arrival time. It was now 12:10 pm, with no luggage on the carousel and no Carl.

Ever since 9/11, no one was allowed to enter the concourses without a boarding pass, so the natural place to meet anyone was where they claimed their luggage. At this subterranean level of the building, no monitors were available to inform Mike of the status of Carl's flight. Marveling at this lack of logic, Mike made his way back upstairs to the ticket counter area. There on a green-on-black screen, he saw the word *Delayed* flashing behind Flight 326. Of course, the screen didn't tell him how long the delay would be. He took a place in the ticket line and it was another twenty minutes before he got close enough to ask the ticket agent when the plane could be expected. By then, the plane had arrived and the snippy little agent looked at him like he was an idiot when she told him the flight had already landed.

Mike ran across one terminal to the escalators, up one floor, and across another terminal to a down escalator, arriving at the baggage claim just as Carl picked up a soft-sided bag from the carousel.

Carl looked good, better than he had for a year and a half. Obviously the sun and sea air did well by him. It had erased the extra twenty pounds he had drunk onto himself after the accident. It made his six-foot-two-inch frame look taller than ever. A dark tan highlighted his already blond hair which was now bleached to near white. It seemed to Mike that even the limp was not as pronounced. The smile creasing Carl's face was a dead giveaway; he had indeed gotten the captain's card. It was the kind of smile that, at one time, Mike thought he might never see again.

After a whole lot of backslapping, handshaking, and near hopping up and down, Carl said, "Let's go to the boat and celebrate."

"Yeah, well, about that, maybe we should talk first. How about some coffee?" Mike's bruised and battered forehead was showing those little beads of sweat again as he steered Carl to the Starbucks kiosk.

"What did you do to my boat, Mike?"

"Nothing, nothing at all. Did you know you're squeaking? There was what you might call an *incident*."

"I guess saltwater and the hinge on the brace don't mix. What kind of *incident*, Mike?"

"Two lattes, please, one with two sugars in the raw." Mike raised a finger to his lips to indicate it would be best to postpone this discussion until they were away from other people.

Carl replied with a sullen glare and a sort of grunt.

Mike paid and carried the two cups over to the padded bench Carl had plopped onto. They both stared out at the runway and Mike began.

"Carl, the boat isn't there anymore because…." It only took Mike about three minutes to tell the whole story, including emphasizing it had cost fifty dollars to be the nice guy looking out for Carl's best interests. "So, you see, you can't go home. We don't know who is after you or why, but they are, and they knew where the boat was. So I hid it, or at least Meyer did."

"Get it back. I need it to live on. Where am I supposed to go? I'll deal with the bastards if they come. I don't have the money to stay in a suite at the Pfister Hotel, you know."

"You have to be reasonable. They could just stroll down to the dock, toss a firebomb, and stroll on home. No more boat, no more Carl. You can't stay awake twenty-four/seven. The boat is better off where it is. Wherever that is, I don't know, but it's safe."

"Fine, maybe you're right, but where do I live, sleep, eat, you know, those sorts of things?"

"You know I'd take you in, but all I have is a back-breaker fold out." Mike stared at Carl, who guessed what he was thinking.

"No way, never, never ever, we have to come up with something else, never!"

"Come on, be a little flexible here. It's just till I get paid or your disability comes in. The boat kid damn near tapped me out. You going to call or should I?"

The glare in Carl's eye was the answer. He knew Mike was right, of course, but moving in with his mom in an old folks' home, even temporarily, was more than anyone should have to endure. He lifted his eyes to the ceiling and said "Why me" as Mike dialed Maggie.

When the phone rang the third time, Mike tossed the phone in Carl's general direction, then stood with a jerk, turned away, and strolled nonchalantly to the men's room.

"Hi Mom, how goes it? Yeah, just got in. You got a few minutes? Thought I would drop by. Sure, he's here. Why don't I bring him along? Count on it. See you in a bit."

Fumbling for cash to pay the parking lot attendant, Mike was still fighting the good fight. "Okay, I'll drive you there, but I'm not going in. She's waiting to pounce on me. I can feel it. She knew I was lying to her and now we're going to confirm it."

As they merged onto I-94, they passed a fender-bender between a gravel truck and a minivan and it came to Mike: the thing he couldn't remember about Carl's accident.

"There were no skid marks. The driver of the semi never meant to stop, he meant to hit you as hard as he could," said Mike.

Carl didn't reply as Mike drove on. He thought about what had happened that night. He could remember dinner with Lauren, leaving the restaurant, driving to within a block of her place, and then never seeing Lauren again.

Mike pulled the car into the lot at Maggie's assisted living center, Fern Hill. He left the motor running, intending a quick getaway once Carl got out, but Carl was on to him and didn't move.

"I'm not going in," said Mike.

"Quit whining, you sissy. What can she do to you? She might even be grateful you looked out for me when I was out of town."

"She'll give me *the look*, that's what; then she'll say, 'I knew it, you were lying and I knew it.' Then comes the forlorn old lady act; she can play me like a cheap banjo and she knows it. After all that, she'll hold it over my head till she needs something. Then she'll haul it back out with a vengeance. How'd you ever come up with a mother like her?"

"I bought her off of eBay, you idiot. Get out of the car, we're going in."

Maggie opened the door before they had a chance to ring the bell and gave Carl a big hug while she raised an eyebrow in Mike's direction. She lowered herself into a huge armchair in front of a twenty-one-inch flat screen monitor and placed her wireless keyboard onto her lap.

"Did you get what you went for?"

"Yup, Mom, first try." Carl handed her the card to examine.

"This is it? Carl, I could have printed one of these up in about two minutes."

"Yeah, I know, but this one is bought, paid for, and *legal*." Carl saw the slightest hint of an upturn at the corners of Maggie's mouth as she handed it back. It was plain she was teasing and was just as pleased as he was.

Maggie turned her gaze to Mike and fixed him with a stare capable of chilling wine. "What have you been up to lately, my near second son?"

Mike turned to look at Carl for the split-second it took to see Carl nod his head ever so slightly. He looked at Maggie, took a deep breath, and the floodgates opened. He was actually surprised at how easy it was to tell a mother someone who had nearly murdered her son once was more than willing to try again.

When it came to the part about not knowing why or even if John Doe was the only party involved, it got a little tense in the room. While both of the men studied Maggie for a reaction, she sat very quietly with her head down. She appeared to be staring through the keyboard on her lap. Suddenly she stood up and said, "Coffee?"

Not waiting for a reply, Maggie whisked off to the kitchenette. She left the two of them looking at each other, not having any idea what to say.

In an effort to end the awkward silence, Carl called to the kitchen, "Do you think it would be all right if I stayed here for a few days? Just until we can get a handle on this thing. Then I can go back to the boat."

"Keep your voice down. Boarders are against the rules and these walls are like paper."

Maggie was back to normal, as close to a field marshal with a riding crop the two of them would ever live to see. They couldn't help themselves; it made them both smile, but only on the inside, where it wouldn't show.

CHAPTER FOUR
Cold Reality

"So that means Lauren didn't die in an accident, she was murdered," Maggie whispered as her eyes started to fill with tears. "She's gone just because she happened to be in the car when this idiot came to get you. Who are these people? What did you do to them? Why would they want you dead?"

"Don't know, Mom, haven't a clue on any count," said Carl as he reached out and put his hand on hers.

Again she fixed Mike with a stare. "What are you doing about this?"

"In fact, not much. The department has assigned other officers to handle it, since I was on the boat. I was on vacation today, so I haven't been downtown to see what Miller and O'Connor have found out."

"Michael McCaffery, no one in the department can tell when you're working or not. They certainly are not keeping track of your vacation days. Now you get down there and snoop. You be back here at six for dinner and let us know what they know. Go, go, go."

And he did.

Dinner was promptly at six and passed quietly. Mike wholeheartedly took advantage of a rare home-cooked meal. He kept his mouth shut when he wasn't stuffing it with meatloaf and mashed potatoes.

After coffee was poured, Maggie and Carl turned to Mike, waiting to hear what, if anything, he had learned at the sheriff's department.

"Miller is sitting there by his phone staring at it. I tell you, it was strange. He never even blinked, he just stared. I don't think they've made any connection yet. I heard from Dale, the janitor, that the boss is on them wholesale to find out who John Doe is. I'm betting Miller and O'Connor are pinning all their hopes on the FBI print database. I guess we are too. If they can find a print match for us, we can start looking into this guy's life. Until we find out who he really is, he may as well be a ghost."

For a split second Maggie studied the faces of the two men. She took in a deep breath and said, "Then I think we have to get busy and help these two helpless officers."

The small dining area of Maggie's apartment took on the tone of a war room. Assignments were agreed upon by each of them to assure there would be no duplication of effort.

Carl was to sneak over to Meyer's boat yard to board *One Fine Day* to recover all of the information about the accident he had kept there. He was sure he had a copy of nearly everything in the original police file.

Mike was to become the best friend either Miller or O'Connor ever had. He was to make certain if they got any leads, Mike would also have them.

Maggie would concentrate on what she did best: using her magic fingers and keyboard to find out all she could about what was going on at the time of the accident and before. She was to see if she could find out why someone was after her son in the first place.

Mike and Carl knew there was no point in expressing their thoughts about involving Maggie in the hunt for the real John Doe. They both knew it would be a losing battle. They exchanged glances letting each other know she would do what she could from the security of her apartment. Under no circumstances did they want her out on the streets with the handgun they knew she had hidden somewhere. The three of them agreed to meet every afternoon at 4:30 to share and analyze what they found out.

The ride out to his boat in Meyer's inflatable shuttle ended in a surprise for Carl. They were within two hundred feet of *One Fine Day* and he hadn't recognized her. A wooden plaque with *Lazy Days* on it covered the name on the stern. Meyer had removed any trace of the fishing equipment normally mounted on her.

"I would never have known her, Meyer."

"That was the idea, son. Even if your new friends knew her before, they wouldn't find her now."

Being back on the boat again, in spite of her new look, was truly coming home for Carl. This was where he belonged now. It was tempting to stay, to fire up the two big engines and just disappear. It wasn't possible now. He had to find out why someone wanted him out of the way so badly they would kill Lauren too.

Carl grabbed the brown envelope he'd come for and a few other items, then climbed back into the dingy.

"Thanks for looking out for her, Meyer."

"Not a problem, son. We kind of cleaned up after your buddy: his things are at the shop for you. We left that black mark that fella made on the stern, in case the law might want to take another look at it. I assume we can cancel the order for cutting the hole in her deck that your boat sitter wanted," said Meyer with a grin.

"A hole? What hole?"

"Never mind, Carl, no harm done."

Carl got back to Maggie's just as Mike arrived. "Someone cut a hole in the deck of my boat. You know why?"

"I can explain that," said Mike. Then he noticed the grin on Carl's face and realized he was being put on. It was a good smile; Mike was glad to see it. The reporting began.

Carl showed them pictures of the accident scene; they all studied them in silence. They proved Mike's theory to a T: There were no skid marks at all. It was obvious the driver of the truck hadn't made any effort to slow down, even after the huge truck hit the side of Lauren's car. They each handled every piece of paper from the envelope and agreed there was nothing else of consequence in any of them.

Mike explained after he'd left them the night before, he found Miller in a local cop hangout and had a few beers with him. Miller had said the preliminary forensics report should be completed by the following morning. Two rounds later, he invited his new best friend Mike to come along to take a peek. While Mike explained to Maggie what they might expect to learn from the report, Carl fell silent.

"You okay, Carl?"

"Yeah, just thinking," he replied.

Maggie heard the words 'just thinking,' but she had seen the look on his face before. It was finally sinking in that Lauren had died for something someone had against him, not by accident or through a fault of her own. The lines around his eyes were changing as she watched him.

When Carl was seven or eight years old, he came to the aid of another little boy on the playground who was the daily victim of bullies. Maggie had been called to school. As she entered the principal's office, Carl was sitting in front of Mr. Highsted's desk, staring at the swollen eye of the head bully. Carl had squinted then the same way he was right now, getting angry as she had very seldom seen.

CHAPTER FIVE
By Dawn's Early Light

Carl banged his knee into the coffee table trying to respond to the third ring of the phone. Forgetting where he was, he greeted the day with a string of expletives that would have made a rap star cringe. His hand landed on top of Maggie's as she lifted the receiver.

"You know, you're better than an alarm clock; you can wake a whole building in one shot. Now I'll spend the entire day explaining who the man in my apartment is. Hello? Well, good morning, Mikey. I didn't think you were capable of waking up before sunrise. What do you need? Hold on, I'll put you on the speaker so Mr. Oaf can hear too."

"Who the hell is Mr. Oaf?"

"One of those jokes you had to be here to appreciate, hon. You're on, dear."

"Rumor has it Forensics was told they were not to leave the building until they'd exhausted every possibility with John Doe. I took a chance they might get something soon and came over with two dozen doughnuts and my boyish charm to snoop.

"Our new M.E., Ron Snyder, told me our stiff had a length of piano wire sewn into the seam of his right pants' leg and a pair of leather gloves tucked into his shirt front–nothing spectacular about them, though, just a regular pair of leather gloves. They're still testing them, but they found traces of some kind of solvent on his hands. It might be like I thought: he may have planned to torch the boat with you in it, Carl. It might be a good idea to have a look around under the water at the dock and see if there is anything there of interest."

"You're thinking if the guy hadn't gotten tangled in the lines when he slipped on the deck he would have lit you and the boat up with a Molotov cocktail or something?" asked Carl. "It's not deep there. I could make the dive myself."

"I know you could go down, but will you come back up with that brace on?"

"I don't need the damn thing to swim. I'm not going to go for a stroll down there."

Maggie interrupted, "Can't we get the Sheriff's Department to send someone down there? I think you'd best stay away from the marina in case there are more of them looking for you."

"I think we can count on there being more of them, Maggie. This guy was a sloppy professional. He wasn't doing this on impulse," said Mike.

"If Miller won't ask for a dive team, let me know and I'll do it at night. There's a chance there might be something down there we want," said Carl.

"Do you two think it may help speed things up if I give Miller or O'Conner a hint or so about your hit and run accident and the fact that it involved you and our corpse?"

"I don't see what harm it could do. They may have guessed already."

Miller showed up at his desk the next morning

more than slightly hung over. He seemed surprised Mike was already in the office.

"Kind of early today, hey, Mike?"

"I didn't want to miss out on anything in case you got the report back early on my sinker."

By the look on his face, Mike could tell Miller had all but forgotten his new best friend of the previous night. Obviously Miller had also forgotten he had offered to share not only the report but also the whole case with him.

"O'Connor is down the hall picking it up now."

Miller and Mike were finishing their second coffee and third donut by the time O'Connor came down the aisle. He had a frown on his face and a manila folder in his hand. "Hi, Mike. Got all that the lab had about the dude you threw into the lake." He grinned at the face Mike made. "It ain't much. We sure could have used more than they are giving us. The old man will be on our butts by ten o'clock and there's really nothing here we didn't already know."

"Can I have a peek?" said Mike. At Miller's nod, he sat down to thumb through the pages. "You know, I got a couple of ideas on this deal, if you want to hear them. Unofficially, of course, since I'm really not even supposed to talk to you two about it."

"We won't tell if you don't. We're struggling here and the powers that be want this cleared up. A body hanging upside down from an ex-cop's boat isn't the kind of P.R. the boss cares for."

"That's kind of my point. You see, I was thinking about what you told me about the fingerprint match to a stolen semi. It wouldn't be the semi that took out

Carl Fletcher, would it? It would be one hell of a coincidence if the same punk who hit him the first time came to his boat to commit suicide."

Mike could almost see the light bulbs go on over the two detectives' heads. It was apparent they had not made any connection at all. They were waiting for the paperwork to solve this thing for them. Mike knew in most cases that hardly ever happened.

"There's one other thing. This solvent on his hands. They don't say here what it was, but maybe he had a firebomb or something. Did the team at the pier ever dive to see if John Doe might have left something in the water when he was hanging upside down?"

The two detectives looked as if they had been simultaneously struck by lightning. They both reached for the phone to request a diver.

"I know where to reach Carl if you want to talk to him. I can run down to the file room to pick up the accident report if it would help, too." Mike knew full well he would come back empty-handed, but what they didn't know wouldn't hurt them. It would give him an excuse to spend some time with Bernadette. He could also explain to his favorite file clerk that it might be a good idea to forget he had already come looking for The File That Never Was.

"Thanks a lot, Mike, we'd really appreciate it," said Miller.

After finding out Bernadette had taken a vacation day, Mike stalled appropriately, then returned to Miller's desk to break the news that the file was missing. He was positive they wouldn't make the connection that the file was deliberately taken, and let it go for now. Mike knew all too well there are only so many times you want to correct someone before that person gets the impression you think he's dumb. Which, in this case, he thought might be true.

Mike managed to make a copy of the forensics report, then wandered to his own desk to let Carl and Maggie know the dive was on.

CHAPTER SIX
4:45 And All's Not Well

The coffee was poured at Maggie's and they were about to tear into the forensic paperwork when the thought occurred to Mike that the divers would find Slip 36 empty when they got there in the morning. No yellow tape, no boat–only that idiot Teddy, who would surely give them a description of the guy who paid him to move it and where. This was not good.

The three of them agreed there was only one thing to do: they had to put the boat back themselves, even if it was only temporarily, without involving any other people, if possible. The more people who became aware of what they were doing, the better the chance of this clandestine investigation blowing up in their faces.

The original plan was for Carl and Mike to go out in a borrowed dinghy, with Carl moving the boat back to Slip 36. Carl would then stay on board overnight in case someone came looking for him or the boat. Mike vetoed the plan before the last words were out of Carl's mouth. His plan substituted himself for Carl, since he was licensed to carry a gun and local law enforcement knew he had been living on the boat anyway. At that point, Maggie reminded them both that Mike didn't know anything about operating boats. Plan 3 was a compromise of sorts:

the two men decided they would both go. They were shocked when Maggie appeared between them and the door with a storm jacket on and her customary cloth shopping bag hanging over her arm.

"Mom, what do you think you're doing? You're not going and that's that."

"Oh, but I am, dear. Number Two here has already shown his lack of nautical skills; if anything, at night they'll be worse. He doesn't know his aft from a hole in the ground and I do."

Mike was about to enter into the argument when Carl touched his arm. Mike knew it was already over and held his peace. Instead he opened the door for Maggie and the three of them made their way to Carl's SUV.

Carl used his cell phone to call Meyer, on the chance he would still be in his shop. He wanted to borrow Meyer's dinghy to get them out to the boat. Meyer was not convinced by Carl's story of going fishing in the soon-to-be-dark. He offered to take them out to where the boat formerly known as *One Fine Day* was moored, without a word to anyone.

The parking lot at Benny's had three cars in it as they drove by, so they parked the SUV behind the diner on the far side of Meyer's. The shop appeared to be deserted, but one of the large rolling doors on the bay side was open, so they went in. Meyer was tossing scrap pieces of wood into an antique looking stove.

Meyer turned to them when he heard Mike trip over the rails embedded in the floor, which were used to haul boats in and out of the huge shed for repairs.

"I can't tell you how much I appreciate this, Meyer. It kind of slipped our minds we shouldn't have moved the boat just yet. It could cause some problems if we don't get it back in the slip for a while," said Carl.

"Yeah, yeah. I don't believe we have been introduced, ma'am. I'm Meyer, this is my place, and you are welcome any time at all. Can I get you some coffee? Here, let me get you something to sit on."

"You don't have to fuss over me, Mr. Meyer, I'm just fine."

"The name is Meyer, no Mister necessary. And you are?"

"I'm Maggie; most days I admit the tall one over there is my son. Sometimes I temporarily adopt this one, when he needs looking after."

"I assume this is one of those days, or rather evenings," said Meyer, with a smile wider than what Carl had guessed his face could make without breaking.

Meyer excused himself and went out the large door. He came back a few minutes later and said, "We're set. It's dark."

Carl expected to find the same shuttle he rode the last time. Instead, an antique runabout, whose polished mahogany deck reflected the full moon, floated at the end of the pier. The rumble of an old straight-eight Packard engine disrupted the quiet of the marina as Meyer helped Maggie down next to him in the front seat.

"This isn't too conspicuous," whispered Mike to Carl while Meyer showed off the boat to Maggie like a teenager on a first date. Carl just nodded his head, but he was really enjoying the smile on his mother's face. In the moonlight, she looked like a teenager too, albeit one with snow-white hair. The ancient Chris-Craft sliced through the rippling surface of the lake and Meyer gently rested her against the side of *One Fine Day*.

Carl leaned over the stern of his boat to hand down the temporary nameplate to Meyer in the runabout, then straightened and fired the engines. Maggie took the helm of the big boat and inched it forward to ease the tension on the anchor line so Carl could raise the anchor.

Mike went below at Carl's request to search for the high-powered spotlight they would use to guide their way alongside Slip 36 upon their return. He handled his exit through the companionway with his usual style, and an ample amount of cursing flowed over the surface of the bay.

Meyer's boat slipped away to the rear of *One Fine Day*, then gathered speed, cutting a large arc around them and taking the lead back towards the marina.

With the moon shining over their shoulders, the small armada made quick work of the distance. Soon Meyer's classic runabout was bearing to the left, making his way toward his own pier to tie up the Chris-Craft. Without any advance warning, the chrome horns on the foredeck of his boat blared. Between blasts, he shouted, "Bear off, bear off! They're waiting!"

The last warning was followed by two flashes of

silver-blue from the side of Benny's, aimed in Meyer's direction. Two more quickly followed in the direction of *One Fine Day*.

Carl twisted the wheel hard right while giving the left engine full throttle, sending Mike yet again sprawling on the sole of the cockpit. Mike executed a massive contortion, trying to right himself and reach the holster under his arm.

Carl strained to see Maggie in the dark. She had been on the foredeck, waiting to handle the docking lines; now she was out of sight.

Just as Carl was about to kill the engines to find her, an enormous roar erupted from the boat. A flash of blue lit up the water in front of the boat, then another and another. Carl could hear the windows at Benny's shattering, then shouting, car doors slamming, and the roar of their engines.

"Stop shooting, Ma, they're leaving. Benny's doesn't have any more windows. Mike, you okay? They didn't get you, did they?"

"Nah, I'm all right. What's a few more knots on the head?"

When they reached the end of the pier, Carl turned right toward Meyer's and hoped with all his heart Meyer was there. He wasn't. As Carl turned *One Fine Day* back out to avoid the dock, a light flashed far out in the bay; he headed there with all the speed his boat had to offer.

With the light held high, Meyer stood on one of the forward bench seats and appeared fine. As the bigger boat pulled alongside, Carl could see the beautiful old runabout did not look well at all. One round had taken out the windshield, and the smell of gas was strong in the air.

"Get him a line, Mom. Meyer, tie her on, then board with us. She may explode if you try to restart her," said Carl. The new captain's orders were followed without question. Soon the damaged craft trailed behind *One Fine Day* to Meyer's shop. When they drew near the pier at Meyer's, both he and Carl jumped into the water. They guided the Chris-Craft onto the little rail car used to take it out of the bay to dry storage.

They spent the next hour siphoning gas from the tank and sponged it from the hull of the runabout while Mike walked guard duty around the property. He had his automatic in one hand and, at Carl's insistence, Maggie's cannon in the other.

Carl noticed some cuts on Meyer's hands and face from the shattered windshield glass. Maggie was more than glad to play student nurse with the shop's first aid kit.

While Maggie fussed over him, Meyer demanded an explanation and got the whole thing, in a nutshell, from Carl. He sat quietly and listened. When Carl finished with all he knew, Meyer slowly shook he head and asked, "What next?"

"We still have to get my boat back to Slip 36. You don't have to do anything, you're out."

"Out! Don't be stupid. It appears I have stolen and concealed evidence. I was the only one who suffered any loss in a gun battle, and the bad guys may have a pretty good idea where I live. You call that *out?* You're right, Maggie, these two do need looking after."

What ensued was not so much a battle plan as a defense plan. Carl would, with the help of Maggie, get the boat back to Slip 36. Meyer and Mike were to keep watch from some of the other boats. Maggie then would hold down the fort at the boat shed until daylight, in case whoever left in the cars came back that way. When the diner opened at five A.M., she would get something for all of them to eat. They all agreed: Being shot at made a person hungry.

When Mike handed Carl Maggie's handgun, there was a small ruckus on her part about being the only one who wasn't armed. Meyer grinned. Opening the cabinet behind his desk, he pulled out a box of .357 magnum cartridges and a long-barrel revolver. He handed both to Maggie.

"I know she can shoot. I don't know nothing about you two," said Meyer as he took a 12-gauge shotgun out of the cabinet for himself. "Slugs or buckshot... Decisions, decisions."

"Speaking of shooting," said Mike, "we better take a look at Benny's to see what we should do about the damage there before the dive team gets here."

"I'll come back here to drop off the gun at dawn and see if there is anything we can do, but I think it may be best just to let it go," said Meyer. "I'm sure it will get blamed on the boat vandal and that will be the end of it."

Meyer was waiting at Slip 36 to catch the lines from Maggie when Carl backed the boat in. He told Carl where Mike had left the yellow police tape, then took Maggie by the arm to help her down to the pier and escorted her back to the boat shed. He then found a place to sit in the dark where he could see all he needed to. At dawn, when he saw Maggie head for the diner, he went the other way toward Benny's Bait Shop.

CHAPTER SEVEN
...And Who Are You?

Maggie entered the diner, ordered coffee, and sipped it while she studied the menu to see what she could conveniently carry. She smiled at the waitress, who was obviously staring at her.

"Up kind of early today, aren't we?" the waitress said as she leaned against the counter just to the right of Maggie.

"Not really, spent the night on a boat."

"I heard one motoring around when I opened, was that you?"

"It might have been," said Maggie. She was trying to be as casual as possible without revealing anything to this nosy parker.

"You wouldn't be Mrs. Fletcher, Carl's mom, would you?"

"Not only would I be, dear, I am. But how did you know?"

Sharon Waters glanced down at the cloth shopping bag, then back to Maggie's eyes. "That's kind of a trademark, or so Carl says."

"Oh really? What else has my fair-haired boy told you and the rest of the world about me?" asked Maggie, indignation growing in her voice. She planned to dump the cloth bag as soon as possible. She would get something hip, like a backpack, the first time she got a chance.

"I didn't mean to hurt your feelings or cause any

trouble. He just said if I ever saw a lady with a cloth bag on *One Fine Day*, it was okay, 'cause you were, well, *you*."

"Well, he hasn't told me anything about you," said Maggie, shifting gears to her nosy mother mode.

"Not much to tell, really. I'm Sharon Waters. I work here, and I got to know Carl since he put his boat in next door. That's about it."

Maggie's instinct told her there was more to the story. As soon as this other mess was cleared up, she was determined to learn more about Sharon Waters.

Maggie ordered what she thought was enough food for all of them; it turned out to be more than she could carry in one trip. Sharon's curiosity got the best of her. In no time, she volunteered to help carry some of the bags over to Slip 36. And Carl.

Things were fine until Sharon noticed Maggie's gun, which Carl had left next to the ship's wheel. Just then, Meyer came through the companionway with his shotgun.

"Little late in the season for ducks, isn't it, Meyer?" said Sharon.

"Well, some of us like to get an early start. The early hunter gets the bird, you know," replied Meyer with a sheepish grin in her direction. He passed a panicked look toward Carl.

"I know this is none of my business, but I'm guessing you have a gun too, Mrs. Fletcher," said Sharon.

Maggie didn't say a word. She just looked down at the cloth bag on her arm that she raised ever so slightly.

"Have all of you turned into bank robbers or something? I'm out of here, and I've already forgotten anything I've seen," said Sharon.

Meyer reached out and touched her arm. "There's a good reason for all of this, Sharon. I think you should stay and listen; you may be able to help us."

"I don't think so, Meyer. I think you're all nuts. You're also a lot more dangerous than I ever imagined." She turned to the companionway to leave and bumped into Mike, who was putting his gun back in his shoulder holster.

"Wait, Sharon, I can explain all of this if you give me a second," said Carl. The story was getting longer and harder to explain every day. Carl gave it his best shot, with a somewhat edited version. With some help from the other three, Sharon became a believer. Meyer was the only one of the group she actually knew well, but there was something about Carl that made her want to believe anything he said, and she did.

Maggie announced that, in her opinion, it was time to let the sheriff know what was going on.

"What would that be, Mom. What's going on? I'm out of town and some guy no one knows from Adam drowns climbing onto my boat. That isn't going to get me twenty-four-hour protection; that I can guarantee you."

Maggie straightened and looked her son in the eye. "What about last night, people lying in wait for you, bullets flying all over, what about that?"

"Need I remind you most of the bullets flying around were from *your* gun, which you are not licensed to carry?"

Meyer cleared his throat. "I think I better get over to Benny's to double check none of those bullets are lying around somewhere to be found."

"Thanks, Meyer. I'll be over to your place as soon as the divers leave. We can work something out about the runabout."

"Don't worry about it, Carl. Fixing boats is what I do, remember? See you later."

"Sharon, would it be okay if Mom stayed at the diner while the guys from the department are here? It might keep things simpler in the long run."

"That would be fine, if you have no objections, Mrs. Fletcher?"

"Wouldn't make any difference around here if I did, would it, Carl?"

"Not this time, Mom. No, it wouldn't."

"You know–it's Sharon, right?–I raised one of the most stubborn people I have ever met in my life. I can't figure where he gets it from. You wouldn't happen to be online at the diner, would you?"

"Yes ma'am, broadband and all, in the back room. All yours if you like."

Carl helped the two of them off the boat. As he watched them walk down the pier together, chattering like a pair of birds, uneasiness came over him.

Carl and Mike draped the yellow police tape back around the stern as well as Mike could remember it being.

"I have to get to work, Carl. You need anything else before I go?"

"No, I can handle this end. Could you stop by

tonight? Maybe we can come up with a plan of what we should do next."

"What time?"

"You know dinner is at six."

"Till then, be careful. I'll keep my ears open downtown. By the way, Carl, thanks for bringing the boat back. It could have gotten pretty ugly for me if the boss found out I had moved it."

Carl didn't feel anything needed to be said. He waved a hand in Mike's general direction and went below. Until then, he hadn't noticed that one of the shots from the bait shop had put a good-sized hole in the front of the cabin. It was just to the left of where Maggie had been standing as they neared the slip. While he cleaned up the pieces of fiberglass, he tried to think of some way to keep Maggie out of this.

With nothing else to do, Carl walked toward the bait shop, half hoping to see if Meyer had found any of the slugs Maggie had sprayed over the area. Teddy was at work with a broom which had seen better days. His red hair looked like a fright wig that obviously hadn't been adjusted with a comb since he left his bed.

"Hey, Mr. Fletcher, were you here when this happened?"

"Not here," replied Carl. He had a thing about lying and technically he was out on a boat when the shooting took place.

"Well, if you get a clue, let me know. The boss is really pissed; he thinks his insurance will go up. He's been yelling at me about it like it was my fault."

"Sure thing, Teddy. I'll keep my eyes and ears

open."

It was no great surprise to Carl that a crime scene team would show up at the bait shop. They were not assigned with the divers. They were sent to look into the vandalism done to Benny's overnight. Investigating officer Mike McCaffery led them.

It turned into a reunion of sorts. As usual, there were about twice as many people as were needed. Carl hadn't seen most of them since he'd left the department, so it was almost like old times.

Mike and his crew joined the other group on the pier. It hadn't taken them long to determine the windows were broken, and there was little hope of finding out who broke them or why.

Terry Jeffords from the crime lab waited with Carl in case the divers found anything of interest. "Carl, I didn't know this was your boat when I was here the other day. Boy, she's a beauty. I have some stuff in the van that will take that tar off the deck. If you want, I'll get you some. It works like magic. We used some to get a sample off of John Doe's shoes. It won't bother your fiberglass at all. I'll be right back, no bother."

Mike hurried to get back to the department. He wanted to see if he could get hold of a complete lab report before they met for dinner. Perhaps there was something there that wasn't in the preliminary, which he had seen earlier, or maybe some of the early pages were missing on purpose. The missing accident file nagged at Mike. Someone had made off with that and he wondered if there was someone in his department with something else to hide.

CHAPTER EIGHT
Dinner For...?

Maggie was busy in her tiny kitchen at Fern Hill when the doorbell rang. "Get that, would you Carl? I'm a little busy here."

Carl was expecting Mike when he opened the door. Instead, Sharon stood there. To say Carl was stunned would be an understatement. He had never seen her in anything but the standard pink waitress outfit. With her hair out of the usual braid and wearing makeup, he barely recognized her. Almost hidden behind her was Meyer with a white shirt and tie on.

Sharon flashed Carl a warm smile. "May we come in?"

"Of course, of course, here, grab a seat. Can I get you anything?"

Meyer said a beer would be nice. Sharon asked for an iced tea.

"Be back in a second," said Carl. He almost ran to the kitchen. He was attempting to ask Maggie what was going on, using various hand signals, when the bell rang again.

"Get the people their drinks, dear, and answer the door. Dinner is almost ready."

Carl hoped with all his heart it was Mike at the door, not his Mom's entire bridge club. His prayer was answered.

"Hi guys," said Mike. It became obvious to Carl he was the only one who was not expecting Sharon and Meyer. As she set serving bowls on the table, Maggie declared there was to be no talk of the affair until they had finished eating.

For Carl, the dinner seemed to drag on forever. Between wondering just how many helpings of everything Mike could eat, catching himself staring at the new Sharon, and occasionally being caught staring by her, it was turning into The Dinner From Hell.

After what Carl deemed to be far too many cups of coffee, everyone helped carry things to the kitchen. There, Maggie loaded the dishwasher in her own very particular style.

When they finally filed into the small living room, Carl explained the divers had found a pair of pliers he had accidentally dropped over the side about a month ago and the regular marina trash, but they found nothing of any importance to them or John Doe.

Mike, with all the drama he could muster, rose to explain his afternoon. "First of all, I guess I got a little paranoid after I found out the report from Carl's accident was missing. No one had taken any pages from the first lab report O'Connor had shown me. He just didn't wait for them to print off all the pages. He did show me all of them he had bothered to wait for.

"Starting with John Doe, he is John Doe no more. The print match came back from the FBI. His name–at least, his *real* name–is Thomas Symons. He has a list of priors longer than my arm and more known aliases than priors. His main claims to fame have been extortion and assault."

While Mike had the full attention of his audience, Maggie typed every word he said into her computer.

"Back to the lab report," continued Mike. "The tar Terry Jeffords from forensics wanted to help you take off your ship was exactly what they found on Symons' shoe, all right."

"So what, we know he was on the boat. Hell, it was the last place he ever was," said Meyer. "We can also be pretty sure he wasn't there to tar the driveway at Benny's."

Mike gave Meyer a look and, with an impatient *harrumph*, went on. "That's the point, Meyer. He had to be somewhere there was fresh tar right before he showed up at the pier, or the tar would have worn off his shoes."

"So Symons had a new driveway installed, or cut through a new parking lot on his way to do Carl in. I don't see where the tar gets us anywhere," said Maggie.

"Not quite, Maggie. This wasn't any old tar. It matches almost exactly the formula set by the state for use on highways; this is no cheap-assed driveway tar."

"So he had to have walked on a new road. How do we find out the closest new road to the pier? Chances are, where he walked, someone knows him," said Sharon.

Maggie's fingers were already moving over her keyboard as Carl stared again at the waitress-turned-

Sam-Spade. Who was she, he wondered. He saw her at least three, four times a week. They had talked, but now he realized he had never really seen her before.

Maggie swore, bringing Carl's attention back to the group. "I thought we could get into the Department Of Transportation, but they must block all access at night. To think my tax dollars helped pay for their mainframe and they have locked me out."

Meyer asked, "Won't it be open tomorrow?"

"Don't know, we can hope."

"I have the next two days off. I could drive around the neighborhood and look for any new roadwork," said Sharon.

"That's possible, but if he drove straight to the pier after he walked on the tar, the road could be miles from here," said Carl, and noted the look of disappointment in her eyes.

"It's a time for patience," said Mike. This absolutely amazed Carl. He, more than anyone, knew Mike had so very little of that precious commodity. "We have to just slow down here. Meyer, how many people did you actually see on the dock last night?"

"Well, there were two guys alongside of Benny's. They were lit from behind by the soda machine; they both jumped in the same car when Maggie opened fire. Then another car pulled away the same time they did, fast."

"Possibly the second car was a bystander who was scared off by the shooting, but why would they follow the shooters? My guess is whoever was in the second car came and left with the shooters." Mike started pacing. "Well, they never got a good look at your face in the dark. They do know you sounded the alarm. Is your boat tucked away? Your boat is probably the only way they could identify you."

"I put it inside the enclosed trailer I use to take it to shows. It's locked up tighter than a drum. I did it when the deputy sheriffs were on the pier; I figured our visitors probably wouldn't be around then. If you think about it, they're not sure we can't identify them."

Mike thought about Meyer's logic for a moment, then agreed. "Good point. I think it might be best if you laid low for a while and just kept an eye open in case they come back. Now they know Carl's boat is back where it belongs, they may come back again looking for it. And him. Sharon, you can see the gate to the marina from the diner, right?"

"I guess so, sure."

"Then it's a done deal. You two watch over the golden boy's boat for him."

Carl watched his old partner working. He marveled at how much Mike had changed since they used to ride in a squad car together. Mike had automatically taken charge and was doing the best he could with what he had available.

"Maggie, if you get anything from the Department of Transportation, call me first thing in the morning. Carl's got my cell number. I'll get over to the county garage first thing on my way in to work. For a dozen doughnuts, I should be able to find out where they were all leaning on their shovels for the last couple of weeks. I suggest we get together again tomorrow night and compare notes. Maggie, I'll put some steaks on my Visa if you don't let Carl turn them into ashes."

"It's a deal," said Maggie, her eyes never leaving the computer screen.

As Meyer slipped on his jacket, he asked, "Mike, I wonder if you could give Sharon and me a ride back to the yard. We came by cab. I didn't think it would be smart to let anyone see our own cars, in case someone was watching the boat."

"Sorry, Meyer, I have one of the company cars, lights and all. Can one of you two drive them?"

Maggie was engrossed with her screen. When she didn't answer, Carl said, "Sure. Let me get my keys."

Meyer climbed into the back seat of Carl's SUV and Sharon sat in the front. Carl noticed for the first time she actually had legs as she straightened her skirt over her knees. Knees too. Who would have guessed? And you think you know somebody, thought Carl.

Meyer suggested he and Carl check the marina when Carl stopped the SUV. The two of them took a quick look around the yard, saw no one, and said their good nights as Sharon stepped down from the truck.

"Where to, missy?" asked Carl.

"Oh, I can walk to the diner from here. See you tomorrow, sleep tight."

"But the diner's closed."

"I have a key," which she raised for him to see over her shoulder as she crossed the lot to the diner.

On the way back to Maggie's, Carl thought about

what had happened over the last few days, how up until now all any of them did or thought about was protecting him and the boat. For the first time since the plane from Florida landed, he was actually alone.

Try as he might, Carl could not think of what started all of this. What had he done over a year ago that set someone out to get him in the first place? Something he did was so important someone was willing to kill for it, not once but twice. Whoever it was, was willing to take out anyone who got in the way, so the situation was bigger than a small time loser with tar on his shoes.

Carl had deliberately put a lot of that time in his life out of his mind. The accident, the operations, and what seemed like endless days of therapy. There were pills to wake him up after he took the pills so he could sleep. In spite of the pills, he didn't sleep. There wasn't a position or place that would let him sleep: bed, couch, or recliner. Every few minutes he would doze off from sheer fatigue, only to wake moments later. Even after all this time had passed, he seldom slept more than three hours at a time, never past three in the morning.

When he was in the hospital, he had learned that most fatalities occurred between three and five in the morning. He would lie in his bed listening to people running in the hospital halls. The staff would whisper in urgent tones. After a few buzzers and bells, it would be quiet again.

All of this was coming back to him again, whether he wanted it to or not. Still, the problem must have started before then. What was he doing before that, that made someone want to kill him? What?

Carl lowered himself into the recliner in Maggie's living room. He pulled the heavy metal brace off his leg, his eyes barely closing, as he waited unwillingly for three A.M.

CHAPTER NINE
Soon Comes the Dawn

The next morning, Carl left before Maggie was up. He waited until he was at the dock before he called Mike. Somehow, he still hoped to un-involve his mother and everyone else but Mike from this whole fiasco. Every time he thought of how close Maggie was to the bullet that punched a hole in the boat, his stomach felt like it was trying to do flips. He knew it was probably a futile effort, but he thought perhaps the less Maggie knew, the better.

Carl realized there was nothing he really had to be here for. He walked toward Meyer's shop to see if he could repair the bullet hole for him. It couldn't hurt to ask.

Meyer was behind his desk, mumbling into the phone, when Carl walked in. Meyer appeared to be in no hurry to hang up, so Carl wandered around the shop. He always loved the smell of wood and solvents in the place. A *good morning* to Hank and Chuck, the two men who worked for Meyer, invited Hank's question.

"That fella ever catch up with you the other day?"

"What fella would that be, Hank?"

"He stopped by the day after the other fella went under; he wanted to know which boat out there was yours. I told him where you were. He looked like a cop, dressed like one."

All of Carl's training and experience came back in a flash. The interrogation began, without Hank even knowing it was happening. The right questions came out at just the right pace so Hank told a story only he knew. He never realized he was closer to giving evidence than he ever imagined.

Meyer had been standing behind Carl and heard most of it; height, weight, color of car and so on. It was over as quickly as it had begun. Carl now knew more about who was hunting him than he had hoped for. Hank was either a great observer of his fellow man or just plain nosey. Either way, Carl now had a picture in his mind of someone who would just as soon see him dead.

Carl took a page off of the legal pad on Meyer's desk. He began jotting down some notes, but he doubted he would ever forget any of it.

"That was your mom on the phone. She says you should come home right now," said Meyer, with emphasis on the *now* and a grin.

"You're kidding, right?"

"Not at all. She didn't say as soon as you can or anything like that, she said *right now!* I bet at family reunions she introduces you as her baby."

"Even if it was true–which it is–you're pushing it, here. Did she say why I should come home?"

"She said, and I quote, 'Tell him to be here on the dot'."

"That means she got into the mainframe at the Department Of Transportation. D.O.T. Dot. She loves talking like a spy."

"I wish you had told me, then I could have played too," said Meyer with a smile verging close to a smirk.

With a rude hand gesture and a 'see you at dinner,' Carl left, thinking to himself that he really liked the old fart.

Maybe it was because of Meyer's sarcasm, or just plain stubbornness on his part, but Carl didn't go straight home. He walked over the lot to the diner. A waitress he knew as Shirley got him the cup of coffee he asked for without comment. "Sharon around?"

"Don't think so, off today, probably at one of her classes or some museum."

"She go to the museum often?"

"I guess you would have to ask her, kid. I really wouldn't know."

Carl left half of the coffee and made his way back to the SUV. On the way to Maggie's, he found himself wondering why he couldn't manage a decent conversation with Shirley. It seemed the only people he could talk to were Mike and Maggie. It never dawned on him that for the most part, other than what was necessary, he hadn't spoken to anyone else for the better part of the last two years.

As he had promised, Mike showed up with the steaks at exactly six. Meyer and Sharon soon followed. Meyer's shirt was even whiter than it had been the previous night, if that was possible, and his tie had a new look about it. There was no dress for Sharon this evening; instead, she wore black slacks and a redder-than-red blouse.

In spite of Maggie's previous table conversation

rules, all they talked about was how to go about finding which tar slick Symons had stepped in last and the possibility of finding someone at the site who could give them more information about who Symons was.

"I think it is more important to find why Symons was out to get me in the first place," said Carl as the rest of them searched for a plan. "I can't for the life of me figure out a way to pin down what I have done that is so important that someone wants me dead. It has to be something bigger than a speeding ticket. I'm not even on the force anymore, so it has to be from a long way back. If that's true, why wait until now? Why not come after me again right away?"

Sharon's eyes surveyed the group and settled on Carl. "They thought they had you the first time. From what I understand, you were in the hospital for months; they had written you off. Something has to have happened since you got out of the hospital to make them want you out of the way again."

"But I haven't done anything but work on the boat and go to school in Florida."

"Maybe it's something someone else did or is going to do. It might even be something you don't know you know."

Mike spoke up. "Sharon is right, Carl. I brought a mug shot from a while back and a post-swim shot of Symons to see if you recognize him at all. They're in a folder over there with his records. I hoped you would find something in there you might be able to use to help us tie this whole thing together." Mike turned to Meyer. "Did anyone show up at the marina today?"

"No one unusual," said Meyer. "Same guys chartering, some of the regular boat owners I've seen before. How about you, Sharon?"

"There was one car that did a turnaround in the diner parking lot, then sat on the side of the road for about twenty minutes. People do that sometimes, just to look at the boats. I could just see his fender while he was parked."

"Didn't happen to get a plate number, did you?" asked Carl as he studied the photos.

"I looked when it turned around; it had one of those dealer plates they stick on with a magnet. I can't really tell one car from another anymore, but it had this shaped logo"–She sketched a design with her finger on the table–"and it was kind of copper-colored."

"That's an Acura logo," said Carl. "Too bad you didn't get the plate number."

"Oh but I did, that one and every one that drove into the marina, the diner, and even down the street. When I thought they were acting, you know, strange," she said as she held several pages from a legal pad in the air.

"You are *fantastic*," said Mike.

A blush touched Sharon's cheeks. In an effort to hide her embarrassment, she gave him a little salute. "Just doing my job, Captain."

"Not Captain yet, but someday," said Mike. "I'll take these downtown and divide them up so I can get some help from some of the guys to track them down."

Maggie reached over the table and took the pages out of his hand. "I'll have them done by dinner tomorrow night."

Mike learned the first time he met Maggie never to doubt her. When she said she would do something, it was so. He let the papers go and asked, "What luck did you have with the DOT? I got your phone message and didn't understand it."

Carl and Meyer both smiled. They assumed she had left the same spy-type message she had given them.

Maggie raised an eyebrow in Mike's direction. "Sometimes I wonder if English isn't a second language for you, Michael. There are eleven road construction and repair sites within a ten-mile radius of the marina, sixteen within a fifteen-mile radius."

"Now we know that, what are we going to do about it?" asked Meyer.

Maggie pulled sheets out of the tray on her printer. "I have marked the locations on these maps. I don't think it's safe for Carl to go near them. So it leaves the rest of us to divide them up. We can take a copy of the picture Symons looks presentable on and go to these places to ask if he was ever there."

"I can't do that," said Mike. "This is not an official case. Even if it were, I'm not assigned to it. I can't run around asking people questions for no official reason. If there are any county workers there, they might even recognize me."

Sharon and Meyer both said "I'll do it" at the same time. Maggie was quick to follow. Carl raised an eyebrow. "What are you going to tell these people when they ask why you're looking for someone who knew Symons?"

He was met with silence for a moment, then suddenly Meyer spoke up. "I'll tell them he owes me money for some work I did and I want to find him. ' Course that likely won't work for you two, but I should be able to handle this by myself."

"Well, isn't that great. I'm odd man out here. I have nothing to do but watch the driveway again," said Sharon with enough indignation to get all of their attention.

"Maybe not," said Mike. "I have been thinking about what Carl said. What was he doing back then that started this whole thing? If it's at all possible to get his records from the department for a while, you and Carl could really study them. Maybe you'll discover why all this is happening."

"You want us to break into the sheriff's department?" said Sharon, the disbelief showing on her face.

"No, no. If Carl's file is still in personnel, no chance, but I think I may be able to sort of unofficially borrow it. That is, if they moved it down to file storage after Carl left the department. If I get it, I'll call you first thing in the morning. I'll drop it off at the diner; it's closer to the office. Both of you can check the file and watch the marina."

Maggie was pounding her keyboard and barely, if at all, noticed that everyone including Carl had left. Meyer had ridden with Sharon, so Carl was again alone. He had deliberately turned in the opposite direction when they pulled into the street, and didn't know why. He drove aimlessly for about ten minutes then, oddly enough, found he was passing the diner. Not able to resist the temptation, he parked at the marina.

Carl had the presence of mind to stay in the truck for a while, to make sure he was alone. Then he made his way down to the pier to sit down in the cockpit of *One Fine Day*, just enjoying being there.

When from behind him Sharon said, "I thought you were supposed to stay away from here," Carl nearly jumped out of the boat.

"How did you know I was here?"

"I watch the driveway here. I thought you knew. It's my new part-time job."

"You don't have to do this, you know; it's really not your problem."

"It wasn't until I found out someone was shooting at Meyer; then it became my problem too."

"How's that?"

"Let's just say I owe him. This just may be the time to start paying him back. You know, I knew you would show up here soon. Before you left town, you would sit out here like this almost every night. I could see you from the diner."

"It's where I feel I belong now. I resent the fact I can't stay here, but if I got killed, Mike would really be disappointed in me. I better go. I guess I'll see you for breakfast tomorrow."

They said no more as they walked the length of the pier. Carl climbed into his truck and watched her until Sharon was inside the diner. While he drove back toward Maggie's, he realized he had just had a real conversation with someone other than Maggie or Mike. He talked very easily to the girl in the redder-than-red blouse.

CHAPTER TEN
Too Good To Be True

"I nearly jumped out of my skin when I turned the light on. What are you doing lying here on the floor? Don't you have a home? How long have you been here?" asked Bernadette all in one breath. She left Mike no time at all to answer.

"Is it my turn now? I've only been here about an hour; when the janitor came on he let me in. He didn't have a key for the gate, though."

"It's probably for the best. He could be fired for letting you in this far."

"Well, let's not even think about that, shall we? The old boy meant no harm."

"Nice try on the sympathy ploy, Mike. I know Dale the janitor; he's not a day over thirty. Don't worry, if I turned him in you'd get the axe too. You do know this place is off limits after hours, don't you?"

"Yeah, I know, but I have kind of a special favor to ask. I thought it would be best if we were alone."

"How special?"

"Let's talk personnel files, Bernadette, old files. Files of people who don't even work here any more. Files nobody even cares about anymore, anyway."

"If it would help move this conversation along, you can call me Bernie. Now we better do the newspaper drill. Who? What? Where? When? How? Just a few things I would like to know in case I get fired over them."

"No, nobody's going to get fired over this. This is old news. You ever meet my old partner Carl Fletcher? I guess you wouldn't have; you haven't been here long enough. Great guy, Carl, and he wants me to look at his files. You see, it started about a year and a half ago…."

The story was ever growing in spite of Mike leaving out selected little items, two of which being Maggie's shoot out and Meyer being shot at. When he was finished with the new, edited, and in some ways super-sized version, Mike realized it was a lot more exciting if you were there in person.

"So you see the predicament we're in. We just want to find out what Carl was doing back then to get someone's goat this bad. What do you say?"

"No, Mike, I can't give you Fletcher's personnel files. It would get me fired."

Mike looked like he was starting to wilt.

"The good news is you don't need or want them anyway. The only thing you would find in there that could be relevant would be a complaint filed against him. I'm sure he would remember if that happened. You would want to see his dailies and any incident reports he filed or someone filed about him. The personnel files are just full of private crap. The records you need are a matter of public record under the sunshine laws. You may know something about crooks and catching them, Mike, but you don't know beans about paperwork here. Or the law."

"I guess not, Bernie. But you do. Right now I need you and those files."

Crossing the Centerline

"We'll find them and I'll sign them out for copying, then you can take them with you. When you're done with them, you will bring them back, all of them." The tone of her voice left no doubt that he would do exactly as she commanded.

When she had all of the files gathered, they filled seven white storage boxes, which in turn filled the squad car Mike had signed out. Even with the help of a handcart borrowed from Dale the janitor, it took several trips to get loaded and on the road. Mike drove off toward the diner repeating 'Bernie' under his breath. He liked the sound of it. It was a good day so far.

When Carl arrived at the diner it was nearly empty. A few of the charter boat captains were waiting for the box lunches they had ordered for their passengers of the day. There was a cook in the back Carl didn't know and the formidable Shirley. Not wishing to pass words with her again, he quietly ordered toast and coffee. His order arrived and there was still no Sharon–just more and more coffee. Finally, he couldn't stand it any longer and asked Shirley, "Sharon be in soon?"

"Oh, you the guy she's been out with the last two nights? She's upstairs screwing around with the telescope she bought. She said to send you right up."

His comment, "We're not really going out," was lost amid Shirley's directions to the door. "Straight back, turn right, up the stairs."

Carl could feel ten pairs of eyes on his back as he made his way to the red and white EXIT sign over the door at the back of the diner. The staircase was old, narrow, and steep, the kind of stairs Carl had come to hate since he began wearing the leg brace. They forced him to take each step one at a time with his good leg then drag the braced side after. Just as he righted himself at the top landing, the door to his right opened. There stood Sharon in her usual pink uniform with the wide white lapels.

"I'm sorry about the climb. I could have met you downstairs, but I wanted you to see something." She held the door wide for him to enter what he had expected to be a storeroom for the restaurant. Instead, it was a large room with a wall of windows facing the street and another down the right-side wall overlooking the marina. The other two walls held a huge natural stone fireplace and floor-to-ceiling bookcases.

Carl was trying to take it all in, never expecting anything this palatial over the chrome and formica diner below. Sharon called to him from the corner windows, "Come and see."

Standing in the corner was a large diameter telescope, pointed down toward the street in front of the marina.

"It's kind of big, isn't it? Looks expensive. I could have loaned you a pair of binoculars off the boat."

The sparkle of a little girl with a new toy didn't leave her eyes, in spite of Carl's logic. "I've always wanted one anyway, so rather than get something junky I decided to kill two birds with one stone. Neat, huh?"

"Do you know a lot about astronomy?"

"Not much, but I always figured it's why we are here, to learn all we can," she said as she repositioned the telescope.

The lens was now aimed at the cockpit of *One Fine Day*. "I can read the gauges from here with this thing," said Carl as he peered through the telescope. "I'll have to remember to pull my shades."

"Too late," she tossed over her shoulder as she went to answer the knock at the door.

"You don't want *all* these up here, do you? There are at least nine boxes like this," Mike exaggerated. He had carefully chosen the lightest of the seven boxes for his maiden voyage up the stairs.

"There's that many?" said Sharon. "I didn't think you'd want us looking at them downstairs, so I asked Meyer if we could use his place. He has an elevator. We can just stack them on a pallet, use his forklift to get them in the building, and up they go."

Mike took the box back downstairs and then moved his car next door to Meyer's. While he was doing that, Sharon grabbed a laptop off the kitchen counter, locked up, and then slowly followed Carl as he worked his way back down the stairs.

As they crossed the parking lot Sharon took an audible breath and said, "Does your leg hurt you?"

"Like they always say, only when it's going to rain."

"How long will you have to wear the brace?"

"Whenever I want to walk for the rest of my life."

"I'm sorry."

"I used to be, too–sorry for myself–but I was the

lucky one. I'm here."

"Meyer told me about Lauren. Maybe that's why I'm sorry."

"Yeah, one self-pitying night after a few too many beers Meyer heard all about it. I'm surprised he told you, though."

"I asked him," Sharon said as if that explained all.

Carl wondered about Sharon and Meyer. He wanted to ask her but they were near the boat yard and Mike was waiting.

Sharon went in to let the crew know they had arrived while Mike and Carl put the boxes onto a pallet from the stack next to the door.

"Don't let anything happen to this stuff or Bernadette will have my ass."

"Who is Bernadette and why would she possibly want your ass?"

"You're right; that may have been a little wishful thinking on my part."

Sharon came sliding around the corner of the building, gravel flying from the forklift's tires. "All right, pal, you better move that rolling video game you drive or I'll put it in the lake for you," she said as the huge machine skidded to a stop.

"As you wish, madam. I'll see you guys at dinner. I heard Maggie has something special up her sleeve." With a flash of the squad car's lights and a short blast on the siren, Mike was gone.

Sharon loaded the pallet onto the elevator, pulled a handcart on behind them, and piloted them to the second floor like she owned the place.

"I thought Meyer would be here," said Carl.

"He left at about six this morning for the furthest road-tarring site, then he's working his way back."

"He's really into this deal, isn't he?"

"That's Meyer. He always says there is only one way to do something: all the way."

Bernadette had marked the boxes with sticky notes, so they searched for the most current boxes. Sharon took the dailies and Carl had the incident reports. The reading began with Sharon making occasional entries into the laptop.

Two people were on the hunt, with no idea what the quarry even looked like.

At his fourth stop, Meyer approached a crew of about twenty-one men. One by one he approached the fifteen men who were watching the rest work. By now, he had accumulated as much tar on his shoes and floor mats as John Doe had. "Any of you seen this fella around here? Well, keep the picture. If you see him or remember anything about him, give me a call; here's my card, thanks a lot." So it went, then back into the car and on to the next site.

Meyer had stopped by Maggie's shortly after Carl left. She had printed directions to the sites for him. They chatted as she made a little coffee for the road.

"Do you think we are doing any good here, Meyer?"

"I don't think we're doing any harm, if that's what you mean. It doesn't appear anyone downtown is getting anywhere. Carl can't stay hiding here forever, and he doesn't strike me as the type to cut and run."

"I guess he gets some of it from me. I'm not exactly what you would call a born quitter either. I never wanted him to be one. What do you think will happen if we do find those jokers from the pier?"

"I don't know, but the boys are professionals; I'm sure they have a plan. If they don't, they better get one soon. I also have a hunch this won't stop with the two from the pier, not by a far shot."

As Meyer pulled away from the curb at Maggie's, her sigh was still ringing in his ears. There was nothing he knew of he could do for the pain of a worried mother, no matter how much he wished he could.

CHAPTER ELEVEN
Dinner at Six

Dinner that evening was a total surprise, at least to Carl. Maggie had food delivered from six different restaurants, every ethnic eatery in the area. They ate off of paper plates with plastic knives and forks. As well as Carl could remember, this was akin to savagery when he was growing up. Maggie was never what could remotely be called domestic, but carry-out was extremely rare, and paper plates only appeared at picnics. Maggie looked up to see the dumbfounded look on Carl's face and said, "Things change. I was busy."

Mike looked at Meyer. "Anything?"

"Well, son, you don't get as old as I am without learning a few things. One of them is knowing when someone is flat-out lying to ya."

"And who was that?"

"The foreman on the job out on the road that used to be Highway 83. He damn near dropped his coffee when I showed him the picture. He developed this little tick while we were talking; then he suggested I leave all of the pictures so he could spread them around. The man is so damn dumb, he thought if he got hold of them I wouldn't have any more. I'm so sure he knew something that I didn't even give him a phone number. I didn't want him—or someone else out there—to know how to find me."

"Good thinking. Do you suppose if I showed up

out there tomorrow with my shiny badge he might regain his memory?"

"Not if his amnesia is brought on by fear. I know how to get what we want, though. If he knew our man, so does someone else out there. I just have to follow them to whatever bar they all stop at after work, find one of the several guys who hates his lying ass and bingo, we have a connection."

"Sharp, Meyer. Just make sure *he* doesn't go out drinking with his boys. How about you, Maggie? Anything fall out of that magic box of yours today?"

"Not what we wanted. The license plate on Sharon's parked car was lifted from a car lot in the Falls a couple of weeks ago. The owner notified License and Trust, who in turn filed a report with the state patrol, who apparently couldn't care less."

"Well, we know it's in the county at least. I'll ask the troops downtown to be on the lookout for it. Maybe if I offer a case of beer as an incentive for the lucky guy who finds it for me we can keep it unofficial." Mike turned the floor over to Carl by pointing in Carl's direction with an egg roll.

"We read till my eyes practically fell out. Sharon's got some kind of timeline program we are entering everything into, but it takes a lot of time. Meyer, your place looks like a Boy Scout paper drive gone bad. It will get better tomorrow, promise."

Mike took a bite out of a taco. With a shrug he said, "Well, maybe we'll catch a break. Something like this could take weeks, so patience, everyone. I assume no one showed up at the boat today."

"Not a soul," said Sharon.

"That's good, I guess, but I wonder what they are waiting for," said Mike.

"Carl, you have to come in through the garage from now on. Anyone for dessert?" said Maggie as if her first statement was an everyday request.

"And why would that be?" asked Carl, dreading the two flights of stairs he would have to climb from the ground-level parking garage to Maggie's door.

"The janitor is ratting you out to the manager. They are pretty sure you are a relative and not my boy toy, but they are certain you have stayed over the five-day guest limit."

"What the hell is it to them? You pay your rent, don't you?"

"Of course. But it is a rule, and a rule is a rule. They just don't want the residents running a low-overhead motel in their apartment. I guess I can see their point, in a way."

Carl stared at Mike, who had averted his eyes down to the remaining four tacos on his plate; no help there.

Meyer, in an attempt to cut through the silence, asked," What's on the agenda for tomorrow?"

Sharon volunteered, "I have to be at the diner for the three rushes, otherwise it's more decoding of someone's bad penmanship."

"My reports aren't written that badly and you know it. You just read funny," said Carl. The smile he saw on Sharon's face made it worth being the butt of her little joke. It was really the first time he had seen how her eyes glittered when she laughed, and he liked it.

Mike and Carl were the only ones who knew Maggie well enough to notice she was quieter than usual. When the others had left, Mike asked her what was wrong. Being Maggie, she gave him the usual, "Oh, nothing."

"But there is, Maggie. Out with it. Is it the deal with management?"

"No, Mikey, it's this doing nothing, making no headway. We have no idea where we are or how long this is going to last. I think maybe you should leave town for a while, Carl. Then maybe this will settle down and go away. Sooner or later these people are going to realize we are looking for them, and they will come back after you."

"I know how you feel, Mom. I wish you, Sharon and Meyer had never gotten involved in this. All we wanted to do was move the boat back. Like they say, what's done is done. You can never unring a bell.

"I honestly believe no matter how long I would stay away, this is so important to these people they will always come back until they get what they want: me. I also don't think Meyer and Sharon would quit now if we begged them. They are not the type of people who can quit; it's not their nature. Neither could you, could you?"

Maggie's silence was the reply Carl expected. They both knew what she would have said.

Mike made himself a doggie bag and waved himself out the door. "Call if you find out anything at all."

"Where do you suppose he puts all that food?" Carl wondered out loud.

Crossing the Centerline

"Don't have the slightest idea, son. Make sure you turn off the lamp for a change." The door to Maggie's bedroom closed.

A roll of thunder woke Carl at 7:45 A.M. It was the latest he'd been able to sleep in over a year. He wondered why as he threw on some clothes from the duffel bag he was living out of.

He picked up the cordless phone from the end table, intending to let Meyer know he was on his way. He heard Maggie's voice on the line and set it back down. Carl poured himself a cup of cold coffee left over from the night before, then tapped on Maggie's door, half whispering, "I'm off, Mom."

He didn't wait for an answer. He cracked the apartment door, looked both ways down the hall, and hurried to the garage stairway.

Meyer was already out of his shop by the time Carl had driven there through the light rain. Hank and Chuck were backing the runabout out of a trailer they had moved into the shop.

Hank motioned for Carl to follow him outside after Carl helped them finish moving the runabout. "I may not be a detective like you and your buddy, but I know what made those holes. My guess is you know how they got there. Has the vandal stepped up his program or is this something else? I want to know if we can plan on someone stopping in to shoot up the place, and what's with Meyer? That man hasn't left the building for two days straight in the fourteen years I've worked for him."

"Meyer's boat got shot up the same time the windows got blown out at Benny's. Nobody knows who did it or why. I'm sure it wasn't personal against Meyer, but it wouldn't hurt to keep your eyes peeled for anything unusual."

"You want me to believe it was just a coincidence your boat got hit at the same time? I suppose what you say may be true, but you and I both know that's not all of it. I'm here to tell ya, son, nothing better happen to Meyer or there will be hell to pay. You mark my words." With a final grunt of exclamation, Hank stalked away.

First Sharon and now Hank. Boy, I wish I had Meyer's friends. Carl made his way up the stairs to Meyer's apartment.

It was nearly ten before Sharon came through the doorway. Carl was hand-writing notes similar to those she had entered into the laptop the day before.

"You know, I led a pretty boring life in law enforcement. Other than breaking up a couple of barroom brawls, I really didn't do much."

"That's not the way Mike saw it."

"Mike talks too much sometimes, and his eyesight isn't always too good either."

"Seriously, since you brought it up, I didn't know how to ask, but...did you ever shoot someone, beat them up? Maybe a relative of someone you messed with holds a grudge."

"I had an aunt on my dad's side who used to pinch my cheeks whenever she saw me, but that's about it."

"Cute. Old Stone Face makes a funny. How far

back have we gone?"

"About six months before the accident. And discovered nothing."

"Then we go back further. It has to be here somewhere."

Sharon left for the diner at 11:30; Carl kept working on the boxes with no intention of letting up. At 1:45, his eyes and stomach let him know it was time for a break. The diner was still half full with the lunch crowd. From across the room, Sharon pointed at the back door, then up.

She had left the apartment door open for him and had set two places on the dining table around the corner of the L. Somehow he didn't feel comfortable sitting at the table when she wasn't there. He wandered over to the telescope and slowly swung it toward his boat. There was a partial view of Hank, who–Carl assumed–was fixing the bullet holes. In an open toolbox alongside Hank's right leg, Carl could just make out the handle of what appeared to be a nine-shot automatic pistol. *This place is turning into the OK Corral, for God's sake.* Was he the only one around here not toting a six-shooter?

He didn't notice Sharon entering the room until she stood directly behind him and cleared her throat. "Tell me what you see."

"Hank is on my boat working on those extra vent holes someone put in it for me, I guess."

She led the way to the dining area and sat at the end of the table. Cold roast beef sandwiches lay under serving covers and two bottles of beer stuck out of an ice bucket.

"Is this okay?"

"Better than I could have hoped for," he replied as he twisted the beer caps free.

"Any luck?"

Carl shook his head. "Same thing, different day. I get the feeling we're either looking for the wrong thing or in the wrong place. I hate to say it, but I think we are wasting our time. We need some help from the outside, someone who knows what we should be paying attention to."

"How about Mike?"

"From what I understand, we wouldn't be looking at these things if it was up to him. It was somebody named Bernadette who steered him to this stuff."

"Well, she gave us every word you had written down about every outside contact you had for the last six years you were on the force. What else is there?"

"I don't know. Maybe we should have Mike ask her if she has any other ideas we could be researching."

"I have a couple of hours free; let's go ask her."

"I don't know about that. I know where she is, but I don't know if Mike or his boss would appreciate us messing with the help."

"Come on, you can always say you stopped by for old times' sake. We don't have to advertise why we are really there. Let's take my car; it hasn't been driven for days."

Carl gave in. After he helped clear the table, the two of them made their way down the dreaded staircase. She turned right at the bottom landing and went out the door marked with the traditional red exit sign.

It took a moment for their eyes to adjust to the bright sun that had replaced the clouds of earlier in the day. With the push of the remote on her key chain, an overhead door on a building at the back of the lot started to open up and she asked. "Top up or down?"

The opened door revealed a classic 1967 Jaguar XKE, even redder than the blouse of a few nights ago.

"You drive this on the street?"

"Well, I used to drive it on people's lawns, but they complained."

"You know what I mean. This thing is gorgeous! Aren't you afraid it will get hit?"

"If it does, I'll fix it. If it can't be fixed, then it's junk. Life is too short to separate yourself from the things you love out of fear they might get hurt. What good is a car if you don't drive it? Top up or down?"

"Down, of course."

"Down it stays, that's the spirit." Gravel flew as Sharon made the turn around the diner and onto the street.

There was that smile of hers again, and again Carl wondered, *Who is she?*

He directed her to a municipal lot a half block from the sheriff's department where they could enter the building by way of the garage. There was only one straight flight of stairs to manage, then they walked down a long hallway past the elevators and through the door marked RECORDS,

AUTHORIZED PERSONNEL ONLY.

Bernadette was just sitting down at her desk when they walked in. "Can I help you? Are you lost?"

"I don't think so. I'm Carl Fletcher, Mike McCaffery's old partner. I was wondering if we could have a word with you?"

Bernadette caught herself looking down toward Carl's leg and quickly lifted her gaze, the start of a blush on her face. "I really can't right now. My boss is headed down here. If you can wait about fifteen minutes, I can meet you in the cafeteria on my break."

"Done deal. I'll buy," said Sharon, who had already decided she liked Bernadette.

As they waited in the cafeteria upstairs, a number of people stopped by to say hello, but quickly became uncomfortable, ran out of things to say, and moved on. Carl understood. He reminded them of how vulnerable they were themselves. Besides, once you were no longer in the fraternity, you became just like everyone else in the world.

"I bet you really miss this," said Sharon.

"It was almost my whole life for six years."

"Almost. Not your whole life."

"You're right, not my whole life. It's a slight exaggeration, but it was what I wanted to be from when I was little."

"Why do you suppose that was?"

"Too many cowboy movies when I was young, I guess. I wanted to be the guy, in the white hat, who made everything right."

"From what I've read in your reports, you succeeded, although I didn't see anything in there about doing it forever."

"I guess it's like the song says: nothing good can last forever."

"Maybe the charter boat business is more than you think; it might be a way you can still make things good for people."

Bernadette crossed the room and took one of the empty chairs. "I can only stay a second. The boss is still down there making a mess of the place. What can I do for you two?"

"First of all, thank you for what you have done already, you've been great. I wonder if we could impose again for a little of your time. Sharon and I thought maybe with your experience you could tell us how to find what we're looking for. It wouldn't have to be here; we're having kind of a dinner meeting tonight. If you're available, you would be more than welcome."

"I don't know if I have anything in my book. I would have to check."

"You can just let Mike know, then he can let Mom know and give you directions or a ride."

"Mom?"

"Yeah. Long story, but we've been meeting at her place."

"And Mike would be there?"

"At six, yes."

Trying not to look too anxious, Bernadette handed Carl a ballpoint pen and a napkin. "Give me the address. We'll surprise him."

CHAPTER TWELVE
Surprises for Everyone

The Jaguar top went up as rain began to fall. Sharon tossed the keys to Carl and held back a smile as he babied the car away from the curb.

"I doubt you can break this thing at ten miles an hour, Carl. Have some fun."

Carl drove like he was hauling eggs. The drive back to the diner didn't last nearly as long as he wished, even at ten miles an hour. When he was lining up to the garage door, Sharon stopped him and asked for the keys to his SUV. She told him she needed a bigger vehicle to haul dinner over to Maggie's. A strange woman walking off with his car might give her neighbors something to gossip about. She was out of the car before what she told him had sunk in. When it did, it was too late and she was gone.

Carl drove the car like every driver he hated on the road. As he drove to Maggie's–at twenty miles per hour and hugging the curb–he was certain the engine was making awful noises all the way. He found a spot to park the Jag at the furthest corner of the Fern Hill lot and prayed it was out of harm's way.

"How'd the day go, Mom?"

"Found out more about the bastard that drowned. He had been out of state for six months. He must have come back right before you left for Florida. You may have passed each other in the airport."

"How did you find that out?"

Crossing the Centerline

Maggie tapped the side of her monitor and said, "You don't want to know. You meet people on here who can go anywhere and find anything they want. If they can't find it, they know someone who can. Wonderful invention, this."

"You're going to end up in some federal prison some day, and I *won't* come to see you."

"Oh, sure you will. The only problem I'll have is trying to decide which is the file and which is the cake. I've seen you cook, my boy: it ain't pretty."

"I hear you got out of cooking tonight."

"Meyer called early this morning. He asked if I would be offended if he and Sharon brought dinner. They even offered to do dishes. I may adopt those two."

"I can't figure them out. They seem tighter than family."

"She hasn't told you?"

"Told me what?"

"Hey, it's not my job, you ask them."

Pleading and blackmail wouldn't move Maggie. Carl had just given up when the doorbell rang. Sharon, peeking over a huge cooler, nearly knocked Carl over in her haste to set it down.

"Go get the rest out of your car. When I cook, I don't carry. Meyer was supposed to help, but no one answered at the shop. I thought maybe he was here. Have you heard from him, Maggie?"

"Not since this morning. He's probably still stalking the tar jockeys."

Carl came back in with his arms full of bags. "You ever notice Mike always comes in when the food is done and has to leave before the cleanup is over?"

Just as Maggie said," You know that's not true, Carl," the phone rang.

"Carl here. What? Where? Where is he now? I'll be right there." Carl was already headed for the door as he turned off the phone. "Give me my keys. Meyer's at County General; they brought him in by ambulance."

No one spoke as they ran to the SUV. Carl kicked up his driving speed by about tenfold; they were running through the emergency room door in less than fifteen minutes. By the time they found the correct waiting room, Mike was there cursing the coffeemaker on a table in the corner.

"Where is he, Mike?" Sharon asked, her face milk-white and tears crowding into her eyes. "I need to see him right now."

"Slow down, Sharon, that's not possible. He needs doctors and nurses a lot more than visitors right now. Sit down. Catch your breath. You better take these; the EMTs gave them to me."

Sharon looked at the plastic bag of Meyer's belongings Mike was offering; some had blood on them. Maggie managed to reach out and grab Sharon before she hit the floor.

Mike and Carl laid Sharon down on one of the settees, then Mike went looking for a doctor or nurse. Maggie knelt on the floor next to Sharon, patting her hand and stroking her cheek, not knowing what else she should do. By the time Mike arrived with a nurse, Sharon's eyes were fluttering as she tried to sit up.

"Where is Meyer?" she asked.

As she took Sharon's pulse the nurse said, "Lie still, dear. If you mean the older gentleman who just came in, I'm not allowed to tell you if he is even here. However, if an older gentleman were here, they would probably be taking him to surgery shortly. Are any of you immediate family of the patient who might be going into surgery?"

Without any hesitation at all, Maggie said, "I'm his sister."

The rest of the group were so stunned they couldn't even react.

"I know all about the new medical privacy laws, dear, but in this case, I'm all he has and I think we had better come to an understanding right now. How is he?"

The nurse hesitated, preparing to serve up the standard hospital position, when Mike held his badge just over Maggie's shoulder. He nodded his head and smiled his warmest smile at her.

"You'll have to come with me to fill out some paperwork, ma'am. I'll send someone back to look after you, young lady."

In a short time, a slight, dark-haired girl who looked about thirteen years old appeared and walked straight over to Sharon. "Hello, I'm Dr. Louise Blackman. I understand you're not feeling well."

"I'm fine, I just got a little upset. Do I know you?"

"We've never really met, but I see you at the gym every Sunday afternoon. I think you also drove one of my patients home from my office one day."

"That was Meyer. They're taking him into surgery right now. He had an accident. Can I see him first?"

Mike didn't think it was the right time to correct her about the accident; later would be better.

"I'll go check on him. I'll be right back. You sit right here. Someone get her some water, please. Just wait. I have to talk to the surgeon right now."

Doctor Blackman left, running down the hallway, her white coat flying out behind her like a cape.

Maggie came back shaking her head. "That lie was a waste of time. That stupid woman doesn't know anything anyway. How you doing, girl?"

"Much better. The water helped a lot, thank you, Carl. We should know something shortly. Meyer's regular doctor happened to be here. She's checking with the surgeon and is coming right back."

"So I adopted Meyer as a brother for nothing?"

"Well, you might be able to see him when he gets out of surgery," said Carl.

Mike pointed at the empty spaces on the couch next to Sharon. "I think we all better sit down. There's something you should know before this thing goes any further. This was no accident."

"What happened? Did he have a heart attack?" asked Sharon, growing even paler.

"Sharon, please, just listen. Someone leaving Ziggy's Tavern found Meyer lying in the parking lot bleeding. From what the deputy who took the call could tell, he had been beaten up pretty badly. He was half underneath his Lincoln, unconscious. Near as they can tell, it happened between five and five-thirty. I'm just guessing at this point, but maybe the foreman Meyer was talking about found out he was trying to talk to one of his crew.

"I think the squad that responded is still over there. I'm going over to see what I can find out. Carl, you have my cell number. Call me as soon as you hear anything. Sharon, can I get Meyer's keys out of that bag? I'll have his car taken to his shop. Maybe we can meet at Maggie's later and catch up."

Sharon looked up at Carl as Mike walked away. Carl knew exactly what she was thinking: Bernadette.

"Mom, I have to go back to your place for a minute. Can you stay here with Sharon? She has a phone; call if you need me," and Carl left.

Maggie moved closer to Sharon on the couch, settling into that form of nonspeaking people do in hospitals. They both knew there was nothing that could be said to make it better. Waiting was all there was.

Carl saw Mike leave the parking lot ahead of him, red and blue lights reflecting off the wet pavement. Parking the SUV across the street from the main entrance to Fern Hill, Carl pulled his jacket over his head. Then he ran to the portico protecting the front doors.

Bernadette didn't recognize him until he pulled the jacket down. She was mad enough at that point she considered driving slowly past him under the portico and continuing on her way home. She realized the way he was whipping his head back and forth he must be looking for someone. She assumed it was her, and there was Mike to think about.

Bernadette started her car and moved it from the curb into the driveway, stopping as close to Carl's feet as she could without driving over him. Carl got the message. The power window rolled down; he was smart enough not to lean in.

"Was this some kind of joke? Meet me at my mother's, but there's nobody home?"

"Not even close, Bernadette. One of the people you were supposed to meet is in County General emergency. Mike is over at a place called Ziggy's trying to find out who beat the hell out of him. I know it's a lot to ask, but would you follow me to County? My mother and Sharon are there. Maybe we could still talk for a minute there."

Carl felt her eyes boring into him, sizing him up. Liar or idiot?

"I don't know. Come to think of it, I don't even know you. I probably shouldn't have come here at all."

"Listen, I know it's weird. But you know Mike and he thinks I'm almost all right."

Funny and pathetic at the same time she could not resist. "Let's go," she snapped. The window went up, then she pulled behind the SUV and waited for Carl to take the lead.

When they arrived at the waiting room, Carl had the impression Sharon and Maggie hadn't taken a breath between them since he had left. He knew they hadn't moved.

"Mom, this is Bernadette, she works for the department. She got my old paperwork for us."

"How do you do, Mrs. Fletcher?"

"It would be nice if you called me Maggie, dear; everyone does."

"And if you would call me Bernie, I would appreciate it. Bernadette is a dumb name."

"Bernie it is, but I think Bernadette is lovely."

"Maybe it's not as dumb as it is long. You can't get it to fit into the blanks on any form in the world."

Sharon tried to smile at Bernie, but the best she could do was croak, "We're sorry we left you hanging like that, but—"

"No need to explain. Carl told me about this. Is there anything I can do for any of you? Can I get you something?"

Carl was amazed at the change in the tone of Bernie's voice from when she had tried to run over his foot. "I'll go. What would you like?"

No one really felt like eating, but he persisted. "I'll just run up to the cafeteria and get some food."

He came back down the hall balancing a tray in each hand. He had emptied the vending machines, near the entrance, of sandwiches and snack foods. They ate almost mechanically, with few words passing between them.

Minutes dragged into hours. The TV hanging from the ceiling scrolled continuous CNN news bites. Above it, the same smiling faces repeated their horror stories over and over. When the four of them could stand no more, Carl turned the volume to zero.

"Why do you suppose Meyer's doctor never came back?" asked Maggie. "You go find her, Carl, and bring her back here. Or at least find out what's going on."

Reluctantly, Carl rose out of his chair and headed toward the nurses' station. "I wonder if you could find Dr. Blackman for me. She was supposed to come back and tell us about my uncle."

"Didn't someone tell you? She went into surgery with him. I guess she forgot to let you know. I'll tell her you're waiting when she comes out."

Carl was sure this nurse was supposed to deliver the doctor's message but blew it. His lack of affection for her was growing by leaps and bounds.

Carl caught himself dozing more than once. He woke to find Sharon sleeping with her head on Maggie's lap.

"Carl, you have to take me home. I have an appointment online in twenty minutes with someone who is helping us."

Carl turned to Bernie, "Do you mind staying with Sharon till I get back?"

"I can stay as long as you want; the department owes me personal days by the dozens."

Maggie slowly lowered Sharon's head down to the couch and joined Carl on his way to his truck.

"What can we do about this, son? Now we're getting our friends hurt. I think it's time we cut our losses and put an end to this."

"Mom, we don't know that this deal with Meyer had anything to do with my problem."

Maggie didn't believe that any more than Carl did. She let him know it with a glance in his direction that said more than words.

The rest of the ride was accomplished in silence. Carl walked her to her door, gave her a kiss on the cheek, squeezed her hand, and said, "It will be better tomorrow."

"You've never been much of a liar, son, but this time I don't believe you at all."

CHAPTER THIRTEEN
Revelations

The waiting area outside the emergency room had come to life by the time Carl returned. There were several people in the waiting room now, sitting or pacing. All of them were trying not to look at one another, but obviously wondering why the others were there.

Bernie and Sharon had moved off to a corner. Sharon sent a half smile in Carl's direction and excused herself.

"She get any rest while I was gone?"

"No, she was awake before you cleared the door. We spent most of the time talking. She's really upset. I don't think she could sleep if she wanted to."

"I wish there was something I could do to help her. This is all my fault and I don't see any way I can make it up to her."

"She doesn't believe you're responsible at all. She knows Meyer better than anybody, and she said she heard Mike warn Meyer about going to the bar."

"All the same, I can't help her. I know she and Meyer have some kind of relationship I don't understand. She's hurting so much…."

"She hasn't told you about her and Meyer?"

"No. What should she have told me?"

"I don't think it's my place to discuss this. I hardly know any of you people. You better talk to her when she's settled down some."

It was nearly one A.M. when Mike reappeared. He studied the food tray but decided there was nothing left of interest.

"How'd you make out at Ziggy's?" asked Carl.

"Same as usual. Nobody saw anything, nobody heard anything. What about Meyer?"

"His regular doctor went in to surgery with him. We haven't heard from anyone since."

"They aren't supposed to tell you anything. It's called HIPPA, the new patient privacy act. I could go over there, flash my badge around and threaten to arrest some of them if you like. I don't think it would do much good, might get me fired though. I don't want to come off as rude here, but...Bernie, what are you doing here?"

"I was invited to dinner at Maggie's. Things kind of got screwed up."

Mike turned to Carl. "I didn't know she knew Maggie. Bernie, how did you meet Maggie?"

Bernadette's mouth turned up at the corners a little. "We go way back: six, seven hours at least."

Seeing his line of questioning was getting him nowhere, Mike went to the little vending machine in the corner. "Anyone want something?"

"I just finished my sixth instant chicken soup; no, thanks," said Carl.

Dr. Blackman entered the room with her stethoscope in hand. Everyone in the room stirred in hope of some information about the patient who concerned them. She walked directly over to Sharon and said, "Walk with me a little bit." They headed out the doors into what remained of the rain. "I got to spend a few minutes with James before they put him under. He wants you to bring the blue envelope from his center desk drawer for me."

"I can't do that, doctor. I know what's in there: it's his will. He's not going to die, is he? He's doing all right, isn't he?"

"Listen to me, Sharon. I know what's in the envelope too, and it's not just a will. There is an envelope in there addressed to me. I need you to get it and bring it to me. I'll meet you here at eleven o'clock; we won't need it for the next few hours."

"What is it you're looking for?"

"I'm not certain. I think it may be a living will and a power of attorney that names you. Are you okay? You're looking pale again."

Dr. Blackman led Sharon back inside to the others. "There isn't anything you can do here for a while. Sharon, you go get some rest. Do what I asked, and I'll meet you here at eleven. With that paperwork, you'll be able to get in to see Mr. Meyer in the morning."

The group made a caravan of three as they left the parking lot. Shortly after, cell phones began ringing.

Carl's phone was the third to ring. It was Maggie.

"I'm your mother, and I'm telling you to bring Sharon here right now. She can get the paperwork anytime. Mike and Bernie are both on their way. *Now*, Carl." Then the line went dead.

"Sharon, we're all going to Mom's, don't ask me why. She wants all of us there now."

"Don't worry, it's fine, I'm sure she knows best."

As he made a U-turn, he looked over at Sharon. Her eyes were closed and there was just the slightest indication of a smile on her lips.

Maggie held open the door to her apartment. It appeared Mike and Bernie had arrived just ahead of them. "Hurry in, or you'll wake up everybody in the building."

"What's so important, Ma?" *Ma* only replaced *Mom* when patience was wearing very thin.

Maggie passed printouts to them all. "First things first. This is a complete description of Meyer's injuries with the prognosis of his two surgeons and Dr. Blackman. So much for HIPPA."

Carl stared at the pages like they were in another language. "We have to get a translator for this."

"The last page is the translation. The doctor who shall remain anonymous liberated it for us," explained Maggie.

"I can read the report," said Sharon. "He has a fractured occipital bone, a concussion, three broken ribs, a broken arm, a broken fibula and several contusions and abrasions. I don't see anything life-threatening here. I wonder why he wants me to get his power of attorney to his doctor?"

"I would guess it has to do with you being able to get in to see him. He probably is as worried about you as you are about him," said Maggie.

There was no stopping Sharon's tears, and no one tried.

"You said you had two things for us. What's the second?" asked Mike.

"I found out some things about the road crew

working closest to Ziggy's. The two closest, actually. The state is required to publish a lot of information on whoever gets awarded contracts for that kind of project. There is a ton of information in the stuff I printed off. The most interesting thing is that both of the companies awarded work in that area have the same address. One company is owned by a woman. She got the Highway 83 project because she was considered a minority business."

"What does it mean to us?" asked Carl.

"I have no idea right now, but I'll find out later today. There has to be a lawyer online who'll help out an old lady like me. Go home and try to get some sleep, all of you. Sharon, call and let me know how that old man is doing as soon as you can. Let's plan on dinner here at six if any of you are awake."

Mike and Bernie went their separate ways. Carl drove Sharon back to the boat shop to get the blue envelope.

"Maybe you might want to get some sleep before you take in the envelope. Things look better in daylight, they say."

"I bet I don't look better. It's been a long night."

"Oh, you look as good as can be expected."

"Wrong answer, junior–and good night to you, too," and the car door slammed shut.

As Carl drove back to Maggie's, he remembered why he seldom had conversations with people. He nearly always seemed to say the wrong thing. There had to be some way to take back what he'd just said, but he sure couldn't think of it.

Beat as he was, even the couch at Maggie's

looked good to him. When Maggie woke him just four hours later, he wasn't in bad shape.

"It's Sharon on the phone. She says you stole her car and she would like it back."

"I didn't steal anything. If she can't remember where she leaves things, it's not my fault."

"I don't suppose you noticed the phone is lying on your chest and she probably heard that."

Carl glared at his mother as he felt himself sinking ever deeper into the hole he had dug for himself earlier.

"Morning, Sharon, haven't you slept at all? You don't need your car till eleven."

"Some of us have responsibilities; we work for a living. Who'll feed the masses if I don't open the diner? Bring me my wheels. I have fresh coffee."

Carl grunted "Soon" into the phone and half hung it up. He was trying to roll over for a little nap when he saw Maggie standing next to the couch with his pants in her hands. "Come on, let's go."

"Where are we going?"

"Sharon invited me to breakfast while you were still out like a bad bulb. Come on."

"You people are nuts," Carl said as he tried to push his hair down somewhere near his scalp.

By the time Carl dressed and drove to the diner, Mike and Bernie had arrived, and were sitting at a table in the front window. They watched Maggie struggle to climb out of the Jaguar with a certain amount of amusement.

"You know, Maggie, you were born to that car. You should get one to drive full time," said Mike as she came through the door.

"Mike, you know what they say about smart-asses, don't you? But of course you would," said Maggie.

Mike thought it was a good time to explore the buffet before his mouth got him in more trouble. Maggie took his place across from Bernie.

"How's Sharon doing this morning?" asked Maggie.

"She seems fine, a little tired. She has been working up a storm since we got here."

Carl joined Mike at the steam table. Carl was studying the selection when Sharon passed behind him and whispered, "People your age have to watch their waistlines, remember."

Without turning around, he changed his mind, put the burrito back, and took an apple instead.

When she had a moment, Sharon joined them at the table. Mike said, "You look happier this morning."

"Dr. Blackman called about twenty minutes ago. She had checked in on Meyer. She says he's doing fine. They kept him in intensive care overnight; he'll be moved to a regular room sometime this morning. He can't talk because of the swelling in his face, so he wrote her a note. She was to tell all of us to come up this morning. He's a tough old bugger."

"How soon?" asked Maggie.

"Soon. I have a lady who retired from here about two years ago coming in to sub for me. She loves to work once in a while, just to mix it up with the customers. She said she would stay on as long as I wanted. As soon as she storms in we are off. Eat up, folks, breakfast is on me," and back to her customers she went.

Carl gave up on the apple to join Mike, who went back to the buffet. Maggie and Bernie nattered over muffins and coffee. Sharon's substitute arrived to a shout from Shirley. "Nina! You old bat, how are you?"

Sharon ran to the wiry little Nina, and engulfed her in her arms. "You know I love you, don't you?"

"Sweetie, just get the hell out of my way. You go take care of that ornery old goat." Nina kissed Sharon's cheek and headed for the counter and old friends.

Sharon asked Carl to walk over to the boat shop with her after he put the Jaguar away.

"Sharon, how much are you going to tell them?"

"All of it. I owe it to them. And to Meyer."

"I don't know about Chuck, but Hank and Meyer are pretty close, I guess."

"We all are; what's your point?"

"You may not know it, but Hank has a gun in his toolbox."

"Doesn't everyone? Hi guys, can I have a minute?" Sharon told Hank and Chuck the whole story.

As they left the shop, Carl said, "They took it well, I think."

"Not if you know them like I do. Did you notice how quiet they were? That's not a good sign."

They drove to the hospital alone. Bernie took her own car. Maggie had convinced Mike she could not go to her grave without riding in a squad car at least once.

The group found seats in the lobby. At three minutes to eleven, Dr. Blackman took Sharon's arm and led her to Meyer's room. On the way, she tried to prepare Sharon for what she was about to see.

"I don't want you to get upset. I have put a few extra bandages on to cover up swelling and bruising. He has no idea what he looks like, but it wouldn't help his morale if you fall apart in there. Do you understand?"

"I won't, count on it, but he'll expect me to say something, that's the way we are. Trust me, he'll understand."

"Okay, here we go."

"My God, Meyer, you look like a damn mummy. What some guys won't do to get out of shaving."

Dr. Blackman could see Meyer wince with pain from smiling. "It might be a good idea to lay off the jokes for a few days or you might be taking your meals through a straw a lot longer than you want." The doctor left to meet with the others.

Coffee in hand, Dr. Blackman approached the rest of the group in the waiting room. "You folks can go in for a few moments after we get this paperwork thing straightened out. I'll let you know when. I'd appreciate if you stayed for just a few minutes. Perhaps you could come back this afternoon? He's still a little groggy and tired. He's doing well but he really took a whipping. You can expect a different face for a while."

In spite of the warning, they were taken aback by

the number of meters and tubes surrounding Meyer and his bed. Sharon stood as close to the headboard as she could get. Her left hand rested on top of Meyer's next to an IV needle.

She smiled as they came in. "And we thought he was in bad shape."

"Looks like a classic case of malingering to me," said Mike. "Don't suppose you could get out of bed and drive me home? I'm really tired. Spent most of the night waiting for dinner with this guy."

As Meyer shook his head from side to side he picked up a pen and wrote, "The foreman out on 83 knows."

"Knows what?"

"That's the problem, we don't know what," wrote Meyer.

"Even if we knew what he does, there's no way we can do anything about it. Maggie came up with some stuff we can talk about tomorrow. We have to go now, doctor's orders." Mike and Bernie waved and headed for the waiting room.

Maggie reached out, touched Meyer's arm, and then walked out after them. She could think of nothing to say. Carl was sure she was crying by the time she cleared the door.

Carl placed a hand on Sharon's shoulder. "Sharon, I think you and I should go too. Let Meyer get some rest, and I promise I'll bring you back later."

Sharon directed a glare at him that faded quickly. She knew he was right, so she gently kissed the bandages on Meyer's forehead. She whispered something in his ear and went out the door.

"Can I ask you what was in the last note he put in your hand as we left?"

"He wants me to ask you and Mike what's next?"

Carl whispered to her as they approached the others, "This is way out of hand. I'm putting a stop to it right now."

They gathered in the parking lot at Carl's request, where he told them, "This is the end, kids. Mike, you and the Department can work on figuring out who did this to Meyer. You deal with them. As of right now, I agree with what you've been saying, Mom. I'm leaving town; the rest of you can go back to your lives. Leave the detective work to the pros."

"Michael, tell me honestly, what is the department going to do about this?" asked Maggie.

"Carl knows as well as I do that unless someone steps forward who can identify who beat the hell out of Meyer, nothing. In a few weeks or so the file will be sent down to Bernadette for her to put away. In all likelihood, no one will ever look at it again."

"The hell it will," said Bernie, almost shouting. "I'll sleep with the damn thing under my pillow if I have to until I find out who did this. I haven't even met this guy Meyer before now, but I could see what he means to all of you. Plus what Sharon means to him. It can't end that way! It's not right, Mike!"

They were all taken aback by the normally quiet Bernie's outburst. It also shamed them to a degree; they all knew she was right.

Maggie put her arm around Sharon's shoulder and they all knew it meant she was in until the end, whatever and whenever that might be. Carl shook his head and looked in Mike's direction for support. What he saw was Mike placing his hand on Maggie's back. Carl surrendered when Mike said, "Maggie, we have to find out who is on that work crew and everything possible about them. Can we do it without getting ourselves killed? Is there a way?"

"Count on it. Dinner at six, my place."

CHAPTER FOURTEEN
Whispers

In a complex exchange of keys and rides, everyone got to where they were supposed to be. Carl agreed to pick up Sharon at three to go back to see Meyer.

While Sharon was at the diner, Carl went to Meyer's apartment to review more incident reports. He had been at it for forty minutes when Hank tapped on the open door, invited himself in, and sat on a towel he carefully spread over a bar stool at Meyer's kitchen counter to protect it from dust.

"You finding anything in there?"

"Not so far. I can't see what I have ever done worth shooting me for." Carl still didn't talk about the semi incident if he could avoid it.

"I called the hospital. They said they couldn't give out no patient information. Lady said it was the law. That so?"

"Yeah, it is. I took Sharon there. I'm sorry, I should have let you know how Meyer is when I came in, Hank. I apologize."

Carl brought Hank up to date on Meyer's injuries, assuring him Meyer would be making a full recovery.

"Cops have any luck finding who jumped him?"

"What do you mean, jumped him?"

"Meyer was an Air-Borne Ranger; he's still strong as an ox. There had to be more than one, and even then if he saw it coming they would be the ones in the hospital, not him." Hank patted the top of Meyer's desk where Carl was seated. "You and your deputy buddy don't look like you're doing a lot to find out who did it." The stare he aimed at Carl was obviously a challenge to explain himself. Carl took it.

"The way we have it figured, the whole thing–the drowning, the shooting, now the deal with Meyer–they're all part of the same thing. We just haven't figured out what yet."

"That's kind of obvious. It's why Meyer has us watching your tub twenty-four/seven. Come up with an idea soon, son. Them messing with Meyer was a bigger mistake than they could know, whoever they are." Hank gave one of the boxes a nudge with the toe of his boot. "You know, when you don't find what you're looking for, it usually means you're looking in the wrong place." He got up, dusted the stool with the towel, and left a chill in the air as he closed the door behind him.

That afternoon on the return trip to the hospital, Carl stayed in the waiting room, deciding to let Sharon have time with Meyer alone. She assured him he was welcome, but it didn't change his mind.

Rather than waste the time, he borrowed paper from the volunteer at the desk and made some notes. He tucked them in his pocket as Sharon came back.

"How's he doing?"

"Kind of disappointed you didn't come in. I told him about you respecting our privacy. He thought it was really funny."

"I thought I was being considerate."

"He and I thought you were being silly, but of course it's only two people's opinions. You appear to be afraid of hospitals and sick people. Could it be a throwback to your accident, maybe?"

"What were you two doing in there, psychoanalyzing me?"

"Of course. Meyer doesn't approve of me hanging out with nut cases, you know. The next time you bring me, you can go in there and hash it out with him. That is, of course, unless you're afraid to."

"I will. I'm not afraid to go in there."

"Right. Hurry up, it's almost six."

Mike and Bernie were already at Maggie's by the time Sharon and Carl arrived. Sharon took a seat on the couch. Carl served her an iced tea then settled himself with bourbon and water on the floor next to her legs.

Maggie gave each of them a list of names including all of the union personnel working on the Highway 83 project. "It doesn't have any of the supervisors' or foremen's names. Do any of these names strike a chord with any of you? I was hoping we could find a connection with Carl in here somewhere."

"I don't recognize anyone on here, but it was such a long time ago. I guess we could go through all my old reports again to see if we could find a match there. Sharon, you up for it?"

"We should be able to do a search on my laptop."

"When I worked alone, I kept a list like your computer file. That would cover all of the reports we have already seen."

Bernie cleared her throat to get their attention. "Mike, what would happen if someone downtown found out I used the records computer to gather information on a nonexistent case then let it out to, say, you?"

"I think it would look real bad for a person who has less than a month to go before they're supposed to take their entry exam for the academy." Mike glanced at Maggie. "On the other hand, if a concerned citizen requested the information under the Open Records Act, then you would have to provide them. You don't even need to go to court anymore; you just need the application approved by a sitting judge."

All eyes, following Mike's lead, turned to Maggie. After her remarks about forging Carl's captain's license, Mike was sure this would be a piece of cake for her.

Maggie did a simple search and found the form in six different places on the net. She printed each of them a copy and asked, "Anyone know a judge?"

Bernie's eyes lit up. "I have a cousin who was appointed a temporary justice in the Court of Appeals in Chicago. That's federal, does that count?"

Sharon said, "It's perfect; no one around here would know him from Adam. How do we get hold of him?"

"I have his number in my folio in the car; I'll get it."

Sharon looked down to see Carl staring up at her. "What are you looking at? Did I spill something?"

"I was just wondering…first you read medical

reports like they are written in English and now you know about the Federal Freedom of Information Act law?"

"I like to consider myself well-rounded, thank you."

Carl looked over to the computer at a smiling Maggie. He shook his head and wandered to the kitchen to get a sandwich before Mike ate everything there.

Bernie was already paging through the address section of her folio as Sharon opened the door.

"I know I wrote his new number in here when he called to brag about his appointment. Where is it?" She dropped into a chair, frustration getting the better of her, the pages of the book flying.

"I used to have one of those. I never put phone numbers directly in the address book. I would write them in the note section or calendar pages. If I wanted to save them for later, then I would copy them into the address book," said Carl.

Bernie gave him a look that nearly spelled *idiot* across his forehead. After another tour of the phone book, she wandered over to the calendar pages–and there he was, Bernard Alfano.

"Your name is Bernadette and his is Bernard?" asked Carl. He tried a little revenge joke for the stare he had gotten from her.

"Yeah, well, it's one of the reasons I hate my name. We were born about two days apart, both named after our grandpa. I truly loved my grandpa, but to make matters worse, Mr. Justice here always seems to be two jumps ahead of me in life."

Maggie, one of the few times during the evening, turned from her computer. She looked directly into Bernie's eyes and said, "I doubt he is anywhere as fine a person as you are, and he couldn't possibly be as lovely, dear." With that, she turned back to the screen. "We better get to him soon. According to this press release, his temporary appointment expires in two weeks if the Senate doesn't approve him permanently."

Carl handed Bernie the portable phone. She dialed the Barrington, Illinois number, got an answering machine. "Bernie, this is Bernie, you call my cell number–I know you have it–at eight-thirty tomorrow morning or all the photos I have of you go to the Senate by sundown. No excuse is acceptable."

Everyone noticed the gleam in her eyes, but said nothing until she giggled and said, "God, that felt great."

Mike turned his attention to Sharon and Carl. "Did you two come up with what Carl was working on right before the accident?"

"Actually, the last report we can find I filed was on the Monday before the accident. A teenager, who had his license all of three hours, ran into a parked car. The accident was on Thursday, as I recall. I'm not quite sure."

"Were you off for those two days, on a desk assignment maybe? I can't help you with this; I was in Vegas at the time. I flew back as soon as Maggie called," said Mike.

"You said you had a folio like this. Did you use it every day?" asked Bernie.

"Sure, I used it; I made notes in it, then transferred the things I wanted kept into my reports."

"Do you know where it is now? I've kept mine for years back," said Bernie.

"I guess it was in the wreck. I don't know where it went."

"Everything they could find from the wreck is in the storage cage downstairs," said Maggie. "I'll bring it up tomorrow."

Carl stood and asked, "Where are the keys? I'll go get it."

"Sit down, Carl. I said I would get it tomorrow and I will."

The tone of Maggie's voice left no doubt that Carl wasn't going into the storage area tonight.

Bernie promised to call all of them in the morning to let them know what success she had with her cousin the judge. They agreed to meet at the diner at six the next evening, and disbanded for the night.

As Carl drove Sharon home, they noticed Hank's car hidden between two of the larger boats stored on trailers at the marina. Carl shook his head and said, "I hope he knows what the hell he's doing. I wouldn't want him to get into trouble–or worse–over this mess."

"Oh, you can count on him knowing what he is doing," said Sharon as she returned Hank's wave. "He always knows exactly what he is doing. Do you want to run the computer list against Maggie's list before you go?"

"I'd like to, but I want to go back and find out why Mom got such a bee in her bonnet about the storage area."

"If you want my advice, and I'm sure you don't, let it go. I'm sure she has her reasons. I think you ought to respect that."

Carl took a step to leave, but suddenly turned back, and kissed Sharon on the cheek. "I'm sure you're right again."

"Why, young man, I do believe you're making me blush." She squeezed his hand and he left.

He kept mulling it over as he drove. As Sharon guessed, he was going to talk to Maggie anyway. He came in to the apartment through the garage entrance and managed the stairs only to find Maggie's bedroom door closed. He heard a thud at the apartment door; it sounded as if someone was trying a key in the lock.

Carl grabbed a pan off of the counter and positioned himself behind the door. The clunking and banging continued as the door slowly opened. Carl brought the pot down full force on the box Maggie struggled to carry in front of her, sending it flying to the floor.

"What in the hell are you doing? You nearly crowned me with that thing. My God, there's potato salad all over the place. Get some paper towels."

"I am so sorry, Mom, are you all right?"

"No thanks to you. What are you, some kind of nut? You were supposed to be driving Sharon home. I didn't expect you back for hours. Haven't you noticed she is a beautiful intelligent girl you have the chance to, at least, spend time with? I swear, Carl, there are times when you are too dense to live. If I didn't know better I'd think you were adopted."

"I wanted to talk to you about the storage area deal. You don't usually fly off the handle like that. Are you okay?"

"I was trying to keep you from the ghosts down there; this isn't the right time for them."

"You're telling me the basement of Fern Hill is haunted? I think you're the one losing it."

"Not haunted for everyone, just you. The last couple of weeks, for the first time since you left the hospital, you were functioning like a real human being again. As ugly as this situation has been, at least it has brought you back to life. There are ghosts in this box. I was afraid they might take you back to where you've been hiding for the last year."

As hard as she tried, Maggie couldn't stop or hide her tears. She bent over, opened the lid of the box, ran her hand inside one end, and pulled out a small maroon velvet bag. "Maybe I was wrong, but I thought it best to let sleeping dogs…. Oh, to hell with it." She handed him the bag and ran into her room. He could hear her crying through the closed door.

Carl didn't have to open the bag to know what was in it. He could feel the small gold cross on a chain; alongside it was a diamond ring. He made himself a strong bourbon and water and sat in the recliner with the bag in his hand. That was how Maggie found him sleeping in the morning.

When he woke, the maroon bag and the box were both gone. Lying on his lap was the folio with a sticky note stuck to the cover that read, "Wake up, clean up, get your own breakfast. I could recommend a diner. Mom."

Carl called out to Maggie, meaning to apologize for the night before. He wanted to thank her for trying to protect him from himself, but she was gone. He took her advice. As he showered, he wondered where she could be at six in the morning. You got to love that woman, he thought as the warming water ran over him.

It was nearly eight by the time he got to the diner. Shirley sat at the counter lighting a cigarette. Nina appeared in front of him as he searched the room for Sharon.

"Your breakfast will be out in a minute. Coffee or milk or both?"

"I haven't ordered yet."

"I know who you are. Your breakfast was ordered at five o'clock. I'm supposed to tell you it's the special and no substitutions are allowed. Back to the coffee or milk thing, honey. Make up your mind. I've got customers, you know."

At ten after, both waitresses appeared with two large trays of food in the small room at the back of the diner. Nina cleared her throat loudly enough to be heard for miles, stared in Carl's direction, and pointed to the table full of food.

As Carl rose from the counter to head in her direction, Maggie and Sharon came in the rear exit door, laughing like little girls home from school.

"Hey everybody, Meyer says hi," said Sharon.

"Carl, you should see him. They took some of the bandages off, and does he ever have one hell of a shiner," said Maggie. "I mean, he was never what I would call gorgeous, but you should see him now."

Carl gave her a frown and said, "Aren't we the compassionate one this morning? Out visiting the sick and making fun of them at the same time."

"Carl, I'm your mother. Listen to me: lighten up. He knows what he looks like; I lent him a mirror. He laughed at himself when he saw his mug–well, as good as he could laugh, with all that swelling. He actually can talk a little now, but I guess it hurts a lot."

Sharon avoided this sparring. She busied herself pushing tables together and spreading place settings out. Nina stepped up behind her to whisper loudly so everyone could hear. "He's cute enough, honey, but he's either hard of hearing or just plain dumb. He still hasn't decided between milk or coffee."

"Nina, we talked about this," said Sharon as she gently helped Nina from the room. "He is a friend who happens to be a boy, not a boyfriend."

"All I have to say to you, sweetie, is if you can look at him and even think *boy*, you're even dumber than he is." Nina turned, gave Carl a wink of approval, and nearly skipped on the way to the kitchen.

Sharon's cheeks were bright red as she shouted after Nina, "Go to work, you evil old woman," with a lot less conviction than she had hoped for because she was laughing too hard.

"Mom found the folio and I took a look through it. There was a reason there were no reports for the three days before the accident. I had to use vacation days to go to court to testify."

Sharon looked at him in disbelief. "You had to give up a vacation day to testify? Isn't that part of the job? Catch the bad guys, take them to court, then to jail?"

"It's one of those things a few bad apples spoiled years ago. Some people would show up at court, testify for five minutes, and take the rest of the day off, with pay. This way you still get paid but it costs you the day off, which most of us would rather have than the money. That's why cops hate to go to court."

Carl was surprised he was so hungry. His plate was empty long before Sharon's or Maggie's. He started paging through the folio. Two pages after the day of the accident, he found a triangle of paper that looked like it was torn from the corner of a yellow legal pad. He had, at some time, written a name on it. The name didn't ring any bells, but he remembered where he was when he wrote it: sitting at the prosecutor's table in District Court 1. Why did he write down the name Wiley Tucker?

Carl interrupted Maggie and Sharon. "Mom, do we know any Tuckers?"

"What kind of tucker, son?"

He handed her the little slip of paper with the stranger's name on it.

"We don't know him personally, but I know where we can find him if we want to. He's listed at the union hall for the pavers as a licensed and bonded paving engineer. Where did this come from?"

"I wrote it on the day of the accident, at nine-thirty in the morning."

Maggie's jaw dropped. It grew so quiet at the table they could hear each other breathing.

"Do you remember why you wrote it?" asked Sharon. "Was he being tried that day?"

"No, not him, a woman named Nedderson. She rammed another woman's car on purpose. She felt Mrs. Hickle pulled into *her* parking place at the Kmart parking lot."

"You gave up a vacation day for that?"

"'Protect and Serve,' that's the name of the game. I don't know why I wrote his name. We could check your laptop to see if I caught him jaywalking at one time or another. Maybe I should just drive over to the job site and ask him if he has some kind of problem with me."

"The laptop is upstairs. I'll get it," said Sharon.

As soon as she was gone, Maggie turned to Carl. "You were kidding about going to the job site, right?"

"Of course I was. I think it's possible this Tucker may have been one of the people who damn near killed Meyer. You had best listen to your own advice and stay away from these people, too. We know there has to be more to this than some stupid ticket I wrote. When we find out what it is, we turn the whole deal over to Mike and the boys downtown."

Sharon came back with the laptop booting up as she walked. Sitting down to click a few keys, her face showed the results. There was no Wiley Tucker in her database.

"So what does it mean?" asked Maggie.

Carl took the lead. "It means I was in the hospital shortly after I was in that courtroom, so I had no contact with this guy after the day I wrote this in the courtroom. The reports don't mention a Wiley Tucker. Whatever Wiley Tucker hates me for had to have happened in the courtroom that day or to someone else before it. If someone else is the common denominator between him and me, we don't know who that is. Maybe if I got a look at him it would help me remember what or who we have in common.

"I probably wouldn't have to see him in person. If we could get hold of a picture, that might do it. Hey, Mom, how about I dress like Clark Kent, you be Lois Lane. I'll pretend to interview him while you snap his picture, then we both run like hell."

"I've raised an idiot. He goes from being a recluse to doing a stand-up act while people are shooting at him."

Sharon snapped the laptop shut. "If a picture will help, I know how to get it. Lets go upstairs, I'll show you."

She and Maggie didn't wait for Carl to manage the stairs. When he walked into the apartment, Maggie was giving the place a royal once-over while Sharon dug through a box on the dining room table.

"I found the manual. Help out over here, will ya?" She pointed at the telescope. "It says we have to unscrew the eyepiece and turn on this here adapter where the eyepiece was. Then the digital camera slides into the adapter and there we go."

Once the camera was in place Sharon used the viewer on the back of the camera to focus the telescope on the pier below. There was Teddy, sitting on an overturned pail in front of Benny's. He was washing something from his hands when she pushed the button on the camera. Before they could ask her what she was doing, she had transferred the memory chip from the camera to the desktop computer next to the telescope and Teddy appeared on the monitor. He was wiping red paint from his hands. The picture was so clear you could even read the label on the paint thinner can between his feet.

Carl was all set to make a comment about luring Tucker over to Benny's to take his picture when Sharon said, "Lets load this baby into the back of the SUV. You drive, Maggie, they wouldn't know you or me from Eve. All we have to do is get within a half mile of these jokers and we'll own them."

Carl carried the camera downstairs while Maggie and Sharon stuffed the huge lens in the back of the truck.

"All right, let's have the keys, big boy. You get back inside and join the girls for coffee. We should be back before you know it. Remember, keep your hands off the help in there." Sharon's sense of humor and her smile left no room for argument. Carl waved as Maggie sprayed gravel all over the lot with his SUV.

Carl didn't go back to the diner; he crossed the lot line and found Hank inside the shop, feeding planks through the planer. He waited until the machine was shut down to get Hank's attention.

"I wanted to let you know, we think we have a good lead. It looks like things may be turning our way."

"'Bout time. Where is the joker?"

"I kinda thought you might say that, so that's all I'm telling you for right now. We think we know who, but with a little patience we might find out why. Then we might need your help. You in?"

"Count on it. But it would be nice if you could promise me a few minutes alone with the son-of-a-bitch before your little buddy cuffs him."

"I can't promise you anything, but then you never really know how things may work out. Deal?"

"Deal. Here's my cell number, anytime day or night. One other thing: you best not let anything happen to Gus's daughter, Sharon. As long as she insists on hanging around with you, she's your responsibility, understand?"

It didn't need an answer. Carl nodded his head, turned, and wandered back to the diner. He took a stool at the end of the counter between the kitchen entrance and the cash register. He waited for the abuse he expected from the pink-clad veterans of hash and bash.

Nina passed by. Without a word she set a glass of milk and a cup of coffee in front of him. He was convinced this frail-looking old woman had to have one of the most vicious senses of humor he had ever encountered. He was trying to think of something rude to say in retaliation when a sheriff's cruiser pulled up out front. Mike climbed out of the passenger's side, and a uniformed officer looking to be twelve going on thirteen got out from behind the wheel.

Nina cruised by. "Well, they finally came to get

you, sweetie buttons. I called them over an hour ago about you loitering in here."

"Good, maybe they'll shoot me and I won't have to finish your so-called coffee."

"Funny. Not bad for a guy who can't tell coffee from milk," she fired back as she retreated to the kitchen.

Mike settled on the stool to Carl's left. "Carl, I just talked to Maggie and she told me she and Sharon were on a hill taking pictures of the Highway 83 project. What in the hell is she talking about?"

"I have no control over what those two do. When they get together they become a force of nature. I see you've grown a shadow."

"This is Chris, Chris O'Connor; he's John O'Connor's nephew. They don't want that spread around. He's on his own time. As a personal favor, he has volunteered to chauffer around a particular piece of paper I'm expecting to get from a young lady in five minutes, give or take."

"You mean she got it already?"

"Industrious little thing, isn't she? Her family photo album must be a pip."

Just then, the SUV crossed the front of the diner and headed toward the back door.

Carl grabbed young O'Connor by the sleeve. "Come on, Officer Chris, we're going to train on how to carry heavy things up really steep staircases."

While they labored at getting the telescope back upstairs to the corner window, Maggie and Sharon printed all the pictures from the camera's memory chip.

"How did it go? Anyone see you or give you grief?" asked Carl.

"We were so far away, they would have had to have a telescope of their own to know we were there. Come and see, the pictures are printing now," said Maggie.

They all stared at Carl as he studied the pictures one at a time to no avail.

"I don't see anyone here I recognize."

"Who are we expecting to see?" asked Mike.

Maggie had started her explanation of what they had found and how they intended to use it when Bernie stuck her head in the door.

"Hello, anybody home?"

Mike almost fell over his feet trying to get to Bernie. "You are the winner of the day, girl. Give the court order to Chris here. He's going to push it through so by six o'clock you can assume your official duties and start your search."

"Mike, that's what I've been trying to tell you. We have a name; we just don't know why. Tell him, Carl," said Maggie.

"Obviously I'm way behind here," said Mike. "Give Chris the papers, Bernie, so he can get going. Thanks a lot, Chris, you're a class act. Now let's all sit down and educate the only cop on the case."

Sharon and Maggie brought Mike up to date on the folio, the telescope, and the name on the piece of paper. They explained how Maggie recognized the name but Carl couldn't remember why he had written it down in the first place.

"Let's assume this Tucker is the person who

wants you dead, or at least one of them," said Mike. "If you don't recognize him in these pictures, chances are pretty good you never arrested him. That still doesn't mean someone else didn't, or at least should have."

Mike continued, "Maggie, you check newspaper articles with your computer, find anything on anyone at all named Tucker. Bernie, go to your office to do the same thing. Carl, your folio says you were in court. If you bothered to write this name down, something happened there or you heard about it there. Either way, there must be a record of it somewhere. You wouldn't have carried any other paperwork with you that day, would you?"

"No, I usually carried just the folio; it fit in my suit coat pocket. We couldn't wear uniforms to court, remember. They said it might prejudice the juries."

"Nothing else you might have written on?"

"That would be a real long shot."

"Well take the shot and look around. Maybe we'll get lucky."

"I'll see you at Maggie's at six. We can all swap notes. I'm going to go talk to the crew patrolling the Highway 83 sector; maybe they can help us out."

CHAPTER FIFTEEN
Any News Is Good News

Maggie's research yielded two bits of information for her to share with the group. "I found two articles in the morning paper's morgue mentioning Wiley Tucker. One was about his being ticketed for speeding three days before Carl was in court. The other was about a brawl Tucker was involved in at a bar called Ziggy's a week before the speeding arrest. There was a mention in the last article about possible charges of assaulting an officer, but there were no follow-up stories regarding it."

"That's because it became a non-story shortly after the article was written," said Bernie. "The charges were dismissed less than a week after his arrest."

"That's it, I remember now! That's why I wrote the name down. The judge wanted to talk to the lawyers about some point of law. He asked them to approach the bench and told me to grab a chair away from the stand so I wouldn't hear what they said. I sat down at the prosecutor's table and his briefcase was lying there open with an arrest report lying in it. Someone had stamped DISMISSED on it in red letters. When the DA came back to his table, he slammed his briefcase shut and told me to keep my nose out of official business and get my ass back on the stand."

"Dismissed by whom, I wonder," said Mike.

Bernie paged through a pile of papers on her lap. "The case was assigned to a prosecutor named James Reece. There's no record of the DA's office doing any follow-up investigation at all. He signed off on the case just three days after Tucker was arrested for the fight at the bar."

"Is there some reason in there for dropping the charges?" asked Sharon.

"Insufficient evidence. I made copies of the whole file so the real cop here could explain how this could have happened. According to this part of the arresting officer's report, his partner was transported to the hospital in an ambulance, and the person who hit him did one night in jail and walked."

"Let me see that, Bernie," said Mike. "Carl, you remember Wise, don't you? He was a second shift captain. His name is on the booking receipt. He also filled out the arrest report. I wonder if he's still around. He was getting ready to retire right after you left the force."

"What was his first name?" asked Maggie.

"Everyone called him Will, right, Carl? I don't know if it was for William, Wilber, or maybe it was his full name."

"There are a number of Wises in the phone book, but only one whose name starts with W," said Maggie, the keys clicking like castanets at her fingertips. She handed Mike a page including Will Wise's address and phone number. Mike pulled out his cell phone while he moved into the kitchen where he could hear better.

"Was it Wise who went to the hospital?" asked

Carl.

Bernie did some more paging to find a copy of the EMT's report. "No, it was a Deputy Collins, Rick Collins."

"I know Collins," said Carl. "He has a boat about three docks away from mine. Small world, isn't it?"

"By the by," said Bernie, "I did a little checking on my own. James Reece isn't a DA anymore. He moved to Manitowoc County and ran for the state senate. He moved just in time to make the residency requirement and won in a closer-than-close election."

Mike walked back in the room as he was closing his phone. "No answer at Wise's."

Bernie told him about Manitowoc's new state senator, then asked him, "What does all this mean, and what can we do about it?"

"Well, I guess first we should try to find out what made Mr. Tucker immune from prosecution. Then we need to figure out what, if any, is the real connection between Wiley Tucker and Thomas Symons, our John Doe. I would guess we have to wait until I can get through to Captain Wise to find out what happened at Ziggy's. Maggie, is there any way we can find out more about this Tucker? Like right down to his shoe size?"

"Consider it done, or at least I'll try to have it done in time for dinner tomorrow night."

"Speaking of that," said Sharon, "I never did get a chance to make dinner the night Meyer went to the hospital. How about at the diner, at six tomorrow? As I hear no dissenting votes, the motion is carried."

"Tomorrow is Saturday; Collins is usually on his

boat for the weekends. I could casually stop by and chat with him to see what he remembers about his call at Ziggy's," said Carl.

"Son, I know you better than anyone here, or in the whole world for that matter. You don't do casual real well. Just walk up to the man and–politely, mind you–ask him what the hell happened at the tavern that night," came Maggie's voice from behind the computer screen.

When the others left, Carl turned to see Maggie putting on her coat. "Where you headed, Mom? It's almost nine."

"Thanks for pointing it out, Carl. I always knew you would grow up to be the smart one. I'm going over to County General to make sure that old fart is properly tucked in."

"It's pretty late. Will they let you in?"

"Of course. I'm his adopted sister, remember?"

"I'd like to tag along if you don't mind. I haven't seen Meyer in two days."

Maggie insisted they stop to get Meyer a good cup of coffee. When she and Carl entered the hospital parking lot, Sharon's Jaguar was already parked in the front row.

Most of the tubes and wires had been removed and Meyer had the bed elevated at an angle so he could watch TV. Sharon was asleep in the chair next to the bed, still holding his hand.

"I thought we'd find her here," said Maggie.

Meyer looked toward Carl. "Do me a favor, son, get Nervous Nellie here home safely. She insists on staying until I fall asleep, but she never makes it."

Carl nodded and gently took Sharon's arm; she woke with a start and blinked to gain recognition of who was there. Carl grabbed a tissue from the nightstand and wiped a little drool from the corner of her mouth.

"Come on, little girl. The boss here says it's night-night time."

Before she could protest, Meyer gave her hand a little squeeze and said, "Go."

"Keys, Carl," said Maggie, reaching out to him.

"I could come back."

"No need, I know the way. Don't worry, I'll be fine."

Carl half carried Sharon down the hall until she got her bearings.

"Did you just wipe spit off my face, or was I dreaming?"

"Why, do you dream about spit often? In answer to your question, yes I did."

"You have to admit, I do have my classy moments."

"Most of your moments are classy," Carl said as he helped Sharon into the Jaguar. She didn't hear him and was dozing against the passenger door by the time they were out of the parking lot.

He helped Sharon out of the car and more or less pushed her up the evil stairway. As she fumbled with her keys, Carl asked, "Do you suppose you and I could go out somewhere to dinner–without the others–some day…maybe…when this is all over?"

Sharon managed to get the door open, turned to

him, and gently touched the side of his face. As she closed the door behind her, she said, "Thank you."

"I should have waited until she was awake," he mumbled as he pulled the keys from the door and struggled with the steps one more time.

CHAPTER SIXTEEN
Menial Labors

Carl didn't want to go home to Maggie's couch. When he pulled out of the diner's driveway, he made a right turn into the marina parking lot. The lot was empty and he thought *All you have to do to get a good parking place in this joint is come in the dead of night*. He pulled the Jag in front of the locked entrance gate.

He locked the door on the Jaguar and made his way down the dock to the pier where *One Fine Day* rested. He almost had one foot on the boat when he felt the gun barrel pressed against his spine.

"Put both your hands up behind your head very, very slowly, please. I'm going to step back just a bit, but have no doubt the gun is still here. Now, step slowly onto the dock and turn toward me, very slowly."

In all the time Carl had been in the service and on the force, he'd had a gun pointed at him only once. When he turned, slowly as the voice commanded, he saw the muzzle of a shotgun that appeared to be the size of an open manhole.

"Oh, it's you," said Chuck, one of Meyer's workers, as he lowered the gun. "What the hell are you doing here? Your mom and your partner said under no circumstances would you be coming near this boat."

"You talked to my mom?"

"Sure, she calls us at the shop whenever she leaves the hospital to let us know how Meyer is doing. She just called a minute ago to say Meyer is going to be released tomorrow afternoon. She said we better get the place cleaned up, and you better get all those papers you left around straightened up, too. I put some back in the boxes. Were they supposed to be in some special order, like filed?"

"Yeah, like filed. I'll take care of them first thing in the morning. It's nice to know you fellas and my mom get along. I'm going to stay on the boat tonight so you can head home. I'll take care of things here."

"No can do, partner. I stay until Hank gets here at twelve-thirty. Then I go over to the shop to catch a nap until we start work."

"You two have really been watching this boat twenty-four/seven? I thought Hank was joking when he told me that."

"When Meyer asks you to do something, it's not for laughs. You know, I didn't catch your name when you first started coming into the shop. What is it?"

"Fletcher, Carl Fletcher, and you are Chuck who?"

"Riddle. You like some coffee, Carl? I have a thermos and extra cups."

After Chuck got them each a coffee from a small galley area in the rear of his conversion van, they settled into the front seats.

"Exactly what are you two watching for, other than making sure I obey my mother and stay away from here?"

"Well, it's common knowledge around the area

someone kind of tried to do you in. So the cop you had staying on your boat talked to Sharon about it, Sharon talked to Meyer, and that was it. You're covered. Meyer told us what he wanted right before he ended up in General. We're looking for anything or anybody who happens along, like you did tonight."

"So who's paying you and Hank for this–Mom, Sharon, Mike, or Meyer?"

"Nobody is paying anybody. I told you Sharon talked to Meyer and Meyer said what he wanted."

"One more question, if you don't mind."

"Sure, go ahead." Chuck spoke very slowly. He'd obviously heard about the coffee-milk thing from Nina.

"What is the deal with Sharon and Meyer? Are they related or something?"

Chuck shifted his weight in the captain's chair seat and ran a hand over his face. "I'm not real comfortable talking about Meyer's private life. I'm sure he wouldn't be comfortable talking about mine. If you have questions about him or Sharon, you better ask them."

"You don't know, do you?"

"Would you like another coffee to take on the boat with you? I'll let Hank know you're aboard so you don't get shot or anything."

Carl knew a hint when he heard one. He could almost hear Maggie in the back of his head: 'Go to your room Carl…*now*.'

Carl looked back at the van as he stepped onto the deck. Chuck was dialing a cell phone. Carl was willing to bet twenty-to-one he was calling Maggie.

It felt great to be back on board his real home. Carl flipped the switch for the vent fans, trying to clear out a combination of musty smells and fiberglass resin odors. Someone had finished fixing the bullet holes.

Waves gently rocked the boat. In a matter of minutes, Carl was sound asleep, and so he stayed until voices out on the dock woke him. The sun shone through the portholes and, for one brief moment, life was good again.

He shaved, took a long hot shower, and dressed like a boater would, in shorts, sandals, and a loud quasi-Hawaiian shirt. Carl looked down the dock for some sign that Rick Collins was at his pier. Too early, he guessed. Carl moved Sharon's car into the garage and headed toward the diner. Not seeing Sharon anywhere, he took a seat at the counter. Nina raised an eyebrow at him, nodding toward the milk dispenser. When he frowned, she smiled and poured him a cup of coffee.

"I suppose you're looking for the boss," said Nina. "She left with Maggie about a half hour ago for the hospital."

"When she comes in, would you kindly tell her I'm over at Meyer's, cleaning up and moving my stuff out of there?"

"How can I possibly refuse, when you ask so kindly?"

Hank gave a wave as Carl climbed the stairs to Meyer's place. His fears became reality as he walked through the door. All of the paperwork had been dumped into any old box. Carl had his work cut out for him.

Occasionally he would look out the wide windows on the harbor side to see if Collins was anywhere to be seen, but no luck. Carl had no excuse for not getting the paperwork back in the proper order for Bernie.

Lunchtime came and went, but Carl felt he was too close to finishing to take a break; he would stick to it and get it done. It was three o'clock before the last box hit the pallet. He was about to go down to the shop to ask Hank to take them out to the parking lot when he realized the only transportation available would be the Jaguar. Not the right vehicle to haul seven boxes. He walked to the diner instead.

Sharon was heading out the back door as Carl came in the front. Nina said Sharon was using his SUV to bring Meyer home, and she was to tell him she'd be right back.

"How did she come to have my truck?"

"Sharon had your mom bring it this morning. They have been here since noon, I guess."

"And where would I find dear old Mom?"

"Son, you have to learn to relax a little. She's in the kitchen baking a cake."

"My mother is *baking?*"

"A cake for Meyer's homecoming. Listen, I'm sick of all these questions. She's right behind that door, son. Go talk to her yourself. I have customers who tip sometimes."

Nina stomped off, leaving Carl to wonder what had happened to his world that his mother would be baking. He'd grown up with a lifetime of store-bought birthday cakes. He was in junior high before he realized a cupcake's proper name wasn't Hostess.

"Hi Mom, hear you gave away my car."

"You know, that doesn't even deserve comment. How could she bring Meyer home in that funny little car of hers? She'd have to fold him in half. You should be at my place picking up your things."

"What things would that be?"

"Everything. Clothes, toothbrush, everything. You didn't get the phone message I left you, did you?"

"No. It might be because my phone is in the car I don't have."

"Don't take that tone with me, young man. It's not my fault the manager at Fern Hill was counting the days. You have overstayed your welcome."

"We're being evicted?"

"Not we, son, *you*. I'm not going anywhere. Would you mind finishing putting the frosting on here? I promised Mike I would have my homework done, so I have to get at it."

Unlike his mother, Carl didn't mind cooking or baking at all. He found the frosting job almost therapeutic. It was like mowing a lawn or mopping a floor, something he could accomplish while his mind was free to wander. Carl's thoughts wandered to his boat and the dock, then he remembered he was supposed to find Rick Collins. Good enough; the cake's frosting job looked far better than any Maggie could have done.

Carl tapped on the side of Collins's hull and

roused no one. Teddy was sunning himself against the wall of Benny's Bait Shop instead of watching the till or whatever else he was paid to do.

"Hey Teddy, you seen Rick Collins today?"

"Collins the cop. Sure, he went out to crew on Tad Anderson's big cutter. Hey, maybe Anderson will tick him off and Collins will shoot him."

"What's the problem with Anderson? I don't know him at all."

"You're lucky. There are guys here in the slips who could buy and sell that dink, but they don't throw it in your face like he does. By the way, he asked Meyer to talk to you about tying up your boat bow-in like everyone else. He thinks your way destroys the effect of the view."

"That will be the day, my friend. You notice Meyer never asked me. He knew it would never make it off the ground at all. You got an idea when the wind chasers will be back in?"

"Well, the ones who don't have auxiliary motors, maybe never, if the breeze don't pick up. Anderson always likes to be the first in, so he should be ramming into the dock within the next fifteen minutes or so."

"Five bucks if you call me at Meyer's when he gets in."

"Nah, you don't have to pay me for that, just cause you ain't an Anderson type."

"Thanks, Teddy. We non-Andersons have to stick together."

As Carl walked toward Meyer's boat shed, Sharon pulled his SUV inside the big overhead door.

He hurried as best he could to see if he could help Meyer out of the truck. By the time he got to the door, Hank and Chuck had made a wheelchair appear from somewhere, and Hank was pushing Meyer onto the freight elevator. Carl waited to get on behind Sharon; it was obvious no one but Hank would be pushing the boss.

Meyer didn't realize Carl was there until Hank pulled the chair past him as it came off the elevator into the apartment.

"Well, young man, how have you been? Long time no see. I hear you didn't take my advice and nearly got shot last night."

"Someone must have shaken your memory loose in the hospital; I saw you there last night."

"Oh, then perhaps it was you who came into my room and kidnapped my nurse, Sleeping Beauty here." He gave the blushing Sharon a wink.

Sharon shook the armrest on the wheelchair. "That was a long way to go for a bad joke, Meyer. You best get in bed so we can set up your machine."

Chuck and Hank handled Meyer like they had done it a hundred times. Soon he was in bed with a machine that would gently lift his arms and legs to stimulate the blood flow through them.

Carl asked Sharon for his keys. "I have to go over to Maggie's to pick up my things. I'm past my time limit at Fern Hill. I'll be moving onto the boat tonight. I'll stop back later to help Hank get the papers out of your shop."

"I thought we all agreed you might not be safe on the boat. After what happened to me, I'm sure of it," said Meyer.

"You can stay at the diner. I have two extra rooms. I can make one up for you," offered Sharon.

Meyer stiffened ever so slightly in his new bed. "This could work out perfect, if you wouldn't mind staying here for a while, Carl. You could help me in and out of this contraption for a few days, couldn't you?"

Everyone in the room knew what Meyer's motive was, even Hank, who had previously accepted the assignment, agreed by nodding his head. "Good idea, boss. Chuck and I will start moving the food over here from the diner while you get your stuff, Carl."

"I hope you don't mind," said Sharon, "But Maggie and I thought it would be easier to bring dinner here than trying to move Gimpy here back and forth."

"I don't mind at all. Excuse me, I have to get some things from the boat."

"I'll tag along; you'll be okay, won't you, Meyer?" Meyer made a motion with his hand. Sharon picked up the TV remote from the desk and handed it to him. "A boy and his toys."

With one click, the map on the wall behind the desk parted and a 47-inch screen came into view. "Two hundred fifty one channels; hell of a lot better than the loop tape on the wonders of broccoli they kept playing at County General. Well, get going, or the real food may all be gone by the time you get back."

Sharon and Carl took the elevator down and picked their way through a light drizzle down to *One*

Fine Day. The cloud cover was helping evening along; the photosensitive lights over the piers couldn't quite decide if they should be on or off.

Carl filled a duffle bag as Sharon took a self-guided tour. "This is real cozy down here. I can see why you miss it."

"I'll miss it even more when I have to give it up for good."

"Why would you do that?"

"Now I have the captain's license, I can start doing larger charters, so I'll need the space for gear. A guy has to make a living."

"Where will you go?"

"Don't know. Somewhere close, I hope. I mean near the boat."

"I knew what you meant."

They both jumped when someone pounded on the hull. "Collins is on his boat. Better hurry; he looked cold and wet when he jumped off Anderson's rig."

"Thanks, Teddy. I don't care what they say, you're all right."

"Who says what about me?"

"It was a joke, Teddy; we all love you."

Carl caught the reaction on Teddy's face when Sharon followed him out of the companionway.

"You heading out or would you like to come along?" asked Carl.

"No thanks, I have to get back to the shop."

"I was actually talking to Sharon, Teddy, but naturally you'd be welcome too. I assume you two know each other."

"Of course. Teddy is one of my regulars: cheeseburger, fries, and chocolate milk," said Sharon, smiling at Teddy.

"I get the dock discount," said Teddy with a touch of Barney Fife arrogance.

"Oh really? And how does someone get this discount?" asked Carl.

"You work here, not play. Maybe when you get your first paying customer," Sharon said as she climbed up to the dock. "Which way to Collins' boat?"

Carl didn't know Rick Collins all that well and he wasn't sure how the detective would react to someone digging into his past. A crisp rap on the hull brought Collins flying out of the companionway. "Hey, you know how loud that is down here?"

"Yeah, I sure do; it happens to me all the time," said Carl.

"You're Fletcher, aren't you? I heard you had an accident on your boat while I was gone. What the hell happened?"

"Don't know. I was out of town at the time too."

"The joke going around downtown is McCaffery pushed some guy in and he drowned. Come on aboard, get out of the rain."

"If you believe that, you don't know McCaffery. If Mike would have had to get out of bed to do it, the guy would still be alive. No chance."

"It's sure making life miserable for Miller and his partner. Every day at roll call they have to try to explain why some assassin is wandering around the harbor trying to kill an ex-cop. Their latest theory is he was the boat vandal and he thought you found him out. It got them plenty of laughs, I'll tell ya. Like every guy who kills for money spends his spare time vandalizing boats, right?"

"It's just possible we might be able to help those two out if things fall into place just right."

Collins realized Carl and Sharon weren't there on a social call. "I thought they retired you, and don't you work at the diner? You telling me you know why the stiff was crawling around on your boat in the middle of the night?"

"Not quite yet, but it's possible we could get closer to knowing with a little help."

"What do you need?"

"You were partnered with Will Wise about a year ago, right?"

"I was his partner up to the day he retired."

"Do you know where we could find him now? He doesn't answer his phone."

"Not his phone here in town, no, not for the whole summer. He has a place up near Antigo; he won't come back until right before Christmas. Sometimes he goes back up during the winter to ice fish. I have a number for him up there, but first, why do you need him?"

"We need him *and* you. It's about a collar you made at a bar fight at Ziggy's."

"Which one? We must have had one every week there for a while. There was a road crew working near the bar. They would go to Ziggy's straight from the job, not eat, and drink like fish. That can make for real trouble."

"They're still out in the area, but one time one of you took an ambulance ride."

"That was me. One of those jerks grazed me with a broken beer mug. Will had to draw his gun to get things back in order. By the time our backup arrived with shields and sticks, we got cuffs on only two of them. The others beat it out a back door."

"Did you ever find out what the fight was about?" asked Sharon.

"Yeah, we got a statement from the fella they were pushing around. He said he never saw those two before, but they were hell-bent on getting him out to the parking lot. He thought at first it was a racial deal. That seemed weak to me; half the crew is black."

Carl gathered his thoughts for a moment, then asked, "Do you have any idea why those guys walked the next day, never charged?"

"One of them never went downtown at all. Will cut him loose as I left with the EMTs, 'cause we never saw him actually *do* anything, but we had the other guy cold. I mean, he came right at me in front of Wise. He was a lock, or so we thought. Maybe he had pictures of the DA with a duck in a motel room. By eight the next day he was out of the coop. I know it really cranked Will. Shortly after that, Will put in for his pension. He figured if they weren't going to back us up in the field, he didn't want to do it anymore."

"I can see his point. You don't happen to remember any of the names, do you?" asked Carl.

"Sure. The one I would call the victim was Alonzo King. The one who went downtown was the foreman of the road crew. His name was Tucker. I think he's still out on the project, I'm not sure. When I came back from sick leave, they had moved Will and me out of the district. I think they thought I might go over there, guns a-blazing."

"Why didn't you?" asked Sharon.

"I worked pretty hard to get this job. I like it, and I'm not throwing it away on a drunken puke like Tucker."

"What about the third guy, do you remember who he was?" asked Carl.

"Sure, it was Michael Thomas, or Thomas Michaels, something like that; it was a long time ago. Will put him in the arrest report. He wanted him in the computer so it would pop up if he got into trouble again."

Carl's reaction went unnoticed by the others. "Rick, you got anywhere you have to be for a little while?"

"Actually, I was going to get on some dry clothes and head to the diner. My wife is at a baby shower for her sister in Green Bay."

Carl gave Sharon a nudge and nodded toward the boat shed.

She got the message, turned on her smile, and said, "How about coming with us to Meyer's homecoming party? The food is on me. Change if you like and walk right into the shop. We'll leave the door open for you," said Sharon.

"Homecoming? Where was Meyer?"

"You'll see. Come as soon as you can. We'll go ahead and set a place for you."

CHAPTER SEVENTEEN
Do You See What I See?

The food was arranged on a makeshift table made up of two sawhorses and a sheet of plywood. There was no room to spare on the four-by-eight-foot surface. Hank and Chuck had pressed Carl's SUV into service as a delivery van to cut down on the number of trips between the shop and diner. Bernadette was doing her best to restrain Mike until Sharon and Carl returned. The disappointment shone on his face when he found out he had to wait for Collins too.

"So, Mr. Detective, the question is, how much trouble could we all be in if we tell Collins all we have done so far and he tells your boss?" asked Maggie.

"Won't happen, Maggie. Rick Collins knows about the 'blue wall'; you never squeal on another cop. Besides, we didn't do anything illegal. The worst thing we might have done is withhold evidence in a case which doesn't really exist. If someone asks us what we know, we'll have to tell them."

Meyer insisted on being up in the wheelchair if Collins was coming. Mike and Carl obliged, since Chuck and Hank had filled plates and gone out to resume their sentry duty.

Collins came in the big door and Carl waved him up the stairs. It was hard to tell if the gasp he made when he reached the top was because he was out of wind or because it was the first time he'd seen Meyer since the beating.

"What the hell happened to you? An accident?"

Carl pointed out that they had good reason to believe the same person who had tried to carve Collins up had put Meyer in the emergency room.

"Did they get the bastard?"

"No witnesses. They jumped him from behind in Ziggy's parking lot. It appears to be headed for the dead letter bin, so we thought we would look into it," said Mike.

"I can't believe the son of a bitch could get away with it again. Who's working this downtown?" demanded Collins, his face growing redder by the moment.

Mike ignored Collins' question. "Let's get a bite and then we'll talk. We all think it's more important to find out *why,* than it is *who* right now."

Collins stood and started pacing. "I'll tell you why *who* is important: he's a mean-assed drunk who thinks he can push around whoever he wants to. I think we should put someone in there undercover with a lot of backup and bait the bastard. When he makes a move, make him pay for it."

"We sort of tried that. Our inside guy is the one in the wheelchair over there. We're positive your boy is tied directly to the dude who failed Boating 101 on Carl's rig."

"Mike, I'm a little confused," said Collins. "If you're not on this case, who the hell is the *we* you keep talking about?" Six hands went slowly into the air. The look of disbelief on Collins' face was amusing.

"If the talk downtown is true, if someone is really trying to snuff out Carl, aren't the rest of you taking one hell of a risk here?"

Bernie looked Collins in the eye. "I don't really know him well, but knowing him directly or indirectly, we all think Carl's worth it."

Collins dropped into a folding chair next to the makeshift table as the others filled their plates. He picked up a stick of celery and, without realizing what he was doing, he started methodically tapping his cheek with it.

"If you're not willing to or can't help us, son, we understand. I would appreciate it if you would just help yourself to something to eat, then forget you or we were ever here," said Maggie as she scooped mashed potatoes and gravy onto a plate for Meyer.

"Huh? Who are you?"

"The tall one with the bad haircut is my son."

"The talk at the department is he was a real good cop."

Maggie smiled in Carl's direction. "Just like his father. Perhaps we should have told you, we found out Carl's accident wasn't an accident. The driver of the stolen semi-tractor that hit him was the same person who just happened to fall off Carl's boat at three in the morning."

"No kidding! I'll be damned… So this is bigger than my bar fight or Carl's so-called accident. Carl, what would you like me to do?"

"When we were in your boat, you said your partner put cuffs on two people, but one was a lack-of-evidence deal, right?"

"Yeah, what's your point?"

Nodding in her direction, Carl asked Bernie, "Bernie, would you give Rick a copy of the arrest report you have so he can look it over?"

Everyone else gathered around the table while Mike and Carl watched Collins' expression as he read the report. They saw what they expected to see.

"Where did this report come from?" asked Collins.

Mike smiled at Collins. "We had someone apply for it under the sunshine laws. Why?"

"Carl knows why. There's no mention of the second arrest or the name of who was assaulted in here. I worked with Will Wise for years. If there was one thing he was good at, it was crossing Ts and dotting Is. His reports were poetry. This isn't even close to his handwriting. This is not the incident report from that night."

Trying to hide his excitement, Carl asked in a calm voice, "Are you positive?"

"Not only am I positive, I can show you. They kept me in the hospital for a few days just to be sure I was healing without infection. The second day I was there, Will brought me a copy of the arrest report, framed, half as a joke, half as a souvenir. The thing is hanging on the wall in my den."

"Rick, grab yourself some food and I'll entertain you with a dinner show about reports, how they can change and sometimes flat-out disappear," said Carl.

While they ate, Rick heard the ever-growing story. At the end, as he finished a cold beer, he asked,

"How do I help?"

"The most important thing you can do right now is keep quiet. We have no idea who is involved in this or even why any of this happened. We can't say a word to anyone outside this room. The second thing is to keep a copy of the report in a safe place. If the wrong people find out it exists, I don't know how far they would go to get it. Third, I think we have to get hold of Wise to let him know what's going on. For his own protection," said Carl.

Collins pulled a flip phone from his pocket and hit two buttons; the speed dial reached out to Antigo. He let it ring for a few minutes, then closed it again. "No answer. He doesn't have an answering machine up there or down here. I'll keep at it and let you know when I get through to him. I would like to have him drive down so you can explain this to him, face to face."

"I'd appreciate it. Now you know why we needed to talk to both of you. We have hit a wall; you have the information we need to get going again," said Carl.

"You know, Mike, I would really like to be the one who takes Tucker down when the time comes, if you don't mind. He has always been the one who got away for me."

"Seems only fair, Rick. If this keeps unraveling like it has, there should be plenty for everyone."

Collins promised to call as soon as he reached Will Wise and left them assured he would help any way he could. He asked them to understand that he, like Mike, had to maintain a distance until they had enough hard evidence to open a real case file.

Mike realized, after hearing the conversation between Collins and Carl, that even though his leg was damaged, Carl was still the good cop he had always been. For the first time since the whole affair began, he turned to Carl and asked, "What do you think we should do next, and who should do it?"

It was almost like being partners again. Carl remembered how much he had enjoyed being teamed with Mike and how well they had worked together.

"Well, Bernie should look at her records to try to figure out who would have access to the files downtown to steal and alter them. There has to be a common denominator somewhere."

Mike nodded in agreement. "Carl, could you track down Alonzo King to hear his story about Wiley Tucker? A soft approach, like 'that bastard beat up a friend of mine too', instead of a cop showing up at his door."

"I'll have Mom look him up first thing in the morning. Maybe I can pay him a visit tomorrow."

As they all pitched in to clean up, Mike's cell phone rang. It was Collins; he had reached Will Wise, who agreed to drive down from Antigo on the weekend. He would meet with them whenever it was convenient.

"Friday morning would be great, at the diner next to the marina. Six-thirty? Perfect," said Mike, then he shut the phone and slid it into his pocket.

When Maggie announced she would bring dinner over to Meyer's the next night, Sharon interrupted. "I'll be here at six for the meeting but not for dinner. I have a previous engagement."

Everyone paused to see if she would say what the 'engagement' was. Finally Mike asked, "Heavy date?"

"Oh, not so heavy. I'll drive, Mr. Fletcher. If you don't mind, that is." With that she went down the stairs and out of the building before anyone could comment.

The cleanup done, Maggie helped Carl make up a bed in one of Meyer's spare rooms. "You know, son, it's been a while since you have dated, and Sharon is a little more independent than most girls."

"Mom, it's not so much a *date* as I just thought she might like to eat at someone else's restaurant for a change."

"Please don't tell me you really believe that, or I may have to disown you."

"You see, when I drove her home from the hospital I asked her if she would like to eat out sometime. She never answered. I thought she was asleep. Tonight is the first I knew she heard me."

"Do you have anything decent to wear on a date?"

"It's not really a date, I said. I don't even know where we are going. That's enough. You go home. Call me when you get a line on Alonzo King."

"You want me to go clothes shopping with you? You should really try to make some kind of impression. I mean the best you're capable of."

Carl shouted one last 'go home' as he locked himself in the bathroom to escape her.

CHAPTER EIGHTEEN
Surprises You Might Have Known

Carl awoke to voices outside his door. He slipped on some jeans and a polo shirt, did up the leg brace, and stepped out into the great room of Meyer's loft over the shop. There he found Nina arranging a tray in front of Meyer, who was already in the wheelchair.

"How did you get out of the bed?" asked Carl.

"I was a nurse in a past life, sonny," said Nina. "I was moving patients before you were potty trained. You are trained, aren't you? I hear you're going out on a date tonight. I wouldn't want you to embarrass the girl."

Carl tried to explain it wasn't a real date, but it fell on deaf ears. Nina was occupied in threatening Meyer's life if he didn't eat his whole breakfast.

"Junior, you bring this back to the diner when you two are done. I managed to sneak a little something on here for you too. I probably shouldn't feed him or you'll never be rid of him," she said to a laughing Meyer and left.

"Can I get you anything?" Carl apologized for not being up to help him into the chair.

"You weren't late. It's not even daylight yet. One thing you can do is help me eat all this, or sure as hell Nina will tell Sharon I'm wasting away."

They were about a third of the way through the mass of food when Maggie called. "Got something to write with, Carl?"

"Go ahead, Mom, all set."

"Telephone number is 414-245-7240, address is W239 N4623 Council. Zip, although I doubt you'll need it, is 53089. Got it?"

"Got it."

"Put Meyer on, Son. Shouldn't you be out shopping soon?"

Carl handed the phone over to Meyer and pointed at the plates. Meyer waved his away, so Carl packed the tray up to return it to the diner.

He hadn't thought about his limp much lately until he carried the heavy tray across the gravel parking lot. Limping was inconvenient at times, but suddenly it had become an embarrassment. Panic started getting a grip on him. What was he thinking, asking Sharon out? Surely she had said yes out of sympathy, or because she got along with Maggie so well. He had to think of some way to let her out of this gracefully.

Brian Richards, one of the charter captains who worked out of the marina, caught the door for him. "Morning, Captain Fletcher. Hear you drowned your first paying customer. Can't tell you how many times I wished one of mine would go overboard. Welcome to the trade. I can promise you you'll never get rich out there, but it beats the hell out of working."

"Thanks, and here's a little tip: Don't let them drown until after you get their money."

In all that had happened, Carl had forgotten about the license and the boat as a career. 'Captain Fletcher' sounded pretty nice. Maybe he should get some cards printed in case he ever had the chance to use the boat.

Nina pointed at the kitchen door. As he walked through, Duane the day cook took the tray from him directly to the dishwasher. "Big date tonight, hey?"

"I don't think it's a real date; it's more like dinner away from here."

"Not what I heard. Being the only guy working here, I hear too much sometimes."

"What did you hear?"

"Your mom told me you was goin' shopping and everything."

"My mom. When did you talk to my mom?"

"This morning. I answered the phone when she called for Sharon. Sharon had already left to get her hair done."

After years on second shift, Carl still marveled at how much people got done so early in the day. It was becoming obvious he might have to go on this non-date after all. He needed help, but he sure wasn't going to call Maggie.

Help was right outside the kitchen door, but was it worth the abuse he might have to take to get it? Unfortunately, it was his only choice. *The things I get into.* He took a stool directly in front of Nina.

Nina held up a coffee cup in his direction and he nodded.

"I assume you know more about this date thing than I do, Nina. Where do you think I should take her?"

"*You* take *her?* You have it kind of scrambled. She is taking you to the new restaurant at the end of the avenue."

"She's taking me?"

"The way I heard it from your mom, Sharon said she was going to pick you up, right?"

"Yeah, that's what she said, but–"

"We all talked it over and decided it was a good place to take you, since *you* can't afford to take *her* there. Carl, this is a small world here around the dock. Everyone knows what your last year has been like. We all know what it costs to keep a boat like yours, not to mention–but I will–the money it cost to get your license. Don't be silly about this, son. If she likes you enough to take you somewhere nice for dinner, go and enjoy it. Have you got a jacket to wear? I don't mean the denim thing you wear around here."

"That's really all I wanted to know. How fancy do I have to dress? I'll arm wrestle her at the table for the check, thank you."

Nina walked away shaking her head, muttering something about *machismo* under her breath.

Carl walked to the boat thinking his exchange with Nina had gone well, all things considered; he was still alive. He pulled a garment bag out of one of the hanging lockers and drove over to Dale's Dry Cleaning. There he found out one-hour service did not mean one hour as the rest of the world saw it. It really meant three hours, for an extra five dollars.

Turning the SUV onto Council Avenue, Carl found W239 N4623 was much farther out in the country than he had thought. He crossed the construction work in progress on Highway 83 just south of Ziggy's. When he ran out of W239 numbers, he did a U-turn in a driveway and headed back into the city. His second pass west on Council was no more successful than the first. There was no W239 N4623. He pulled into the lot of a convenience store to dial Maggie and asked her to double check the number. She said she was sure it was correct.

Carl went inside the store and asked the rosy-cheeked grandmotherly type behind the counter for help.

"No, you have the right part of Council, but the numbers don't go that high anymore. That address would have been right on the corner. They took all those buildings down after the fire, when Alonzo King died, oh, it must be about a year ago now. I think all that's left there now is the basement."

"Mr. King died in a fire?"

"No, the fire was after he died. He fell down the basement steps. I heard someone from Mount Zion Baptist Church found him when he didn't show up for the services on Sunday. He was a deacon over there I think, something like that."

An ache grew in Carl's stomach; he knew he had to get out of there as quickly as he could before he shouted, 'He didn't fall, you old fool, the bastards killed him!'

Still, Carl felt obligated to buy something after the clerk was so kind. He got a cup of coffee and a package of highly preserved doughnuts to go. He sat in the parking lot to eat the doughnuts and to absorb what he had just learned.

Carl knew in his heart the tavern fight was just

the beginning of the end for Alonzo King. Knowing *why* was a different matter. What had King done that was so irritating to the paving foreman that he or whomever was behind the murder would kill him for it?

Carl couldn't think of anything he could accomplish on Council Avenue anymore. He had no idea where he should go or what he should do. He had to talk to someone about this. He had to tell someone what he surmised to be true. There was only one person he positively knew would be where Carl expected him to be. He headed for the boat shed.

CHAPTER NINETEEN
Timing Is Everything

The big screen TV was flashing from one station to all two hundred fifty others as Meyer worked the remote with the disinterest of a man totally bored.

"How did you get back in bed?"

"Sharon sent that maniac woman, Nina, over here to check on me, as if I was a child and couldn't be trusted."

"And?"

"I rode the elevator down to see what the boys were up to. You don't suppose they have some signal worked out to let Sharon know what I'm doing, do you?"

"If you want to be paranoid about something, try this," said Carl. He dropped into the swivel chair behind the desk. "Mr. Alonzo King, who we thought was going to help us figure out why the road crew beats up anyone who crosses their path, is dead."

"When did he die?"

"I don't know for sure, but it was a little over a year ago. Just as a matter of interest, you can see your old hangout, Ziggy's, from what used to be his house. It burned down shortly after he died."

"Hand me the phone, son." Meyer winced reaching for it. With visible pain the buttons were pushed. "Maggie, it's Jim. The meeting can't wait until tonight. Get hold of Bernie and Mike, have them come here for lunch. I'll take care of Sharon and the food. Yes, he's here. See you in a bit."

"Your name is Jim?"

"Shut up. Go over by Sharon's and get some sandwiches made. Put them on my tab. Wait, first help me out of this damn bed."

"What do you mean, you helped him out of bed?" accused Nina, slapping Carl's hand as he reached for a sandwich.

"Listen, if Meyer tells me he wants to go bowling, it's a done deal as far as I'm concerned. I not only helped him up, he is shaved, showered, and dressed in his usual bibs and flannel shirt."

"Moron."

"Will you two stop bickering, or I'll stop this kitchen and spank you both," said Sharon. "What does Meyer want with us that can't wait, Carl?"

Carl rolled his eyes in Nina's direction and said, "He told me he would explain when you got there."

It was a quarter of twelve when they saw a squad car roll up to the boat shed. Sharon and Carl crossed the parking lot with a gallon thermos of coffee and nearly enough sandwiches to keep Mike happy.

Hank and Chuck were taking the file boxes off the elevator and loading the squad car with them. Carl and Sharon had to manage on the stairs. Maggie's car door slammed as they reached the landing. They could hear her chatting with Hank as she came through the big doorway.

They served themselves as Carl described the suspicious death of Alonzo King. Mike slipped into his partner mode again and asked, "Any suggestions? Where do we go from here?"

Bernie asked Meyer if he had a big sheet of paper. Much to his dismay, she taped it over the big TV screen. "What do we know so far for sure? Let's get it all down on here to see what we really know, not just what we think we remember."

As everyone contributed, Bernie wrote their conclusions on the paper, then reviewed them aloud.

"One: Carl sees a move to dismiss charges against Wiley Tucker when we know there is an ironclad case against him for the tavern fight.

"Two: As best we can tell, because of this, they, meaning Reece, the DA, and Tucker, want Carl dead.

"Three: They also, for unknown reasons, wanted Alonzo King dead. In his case, they succeeded.

"In my opinion, it all comes down to those two, King and Tucker. Your curiosity put you right between them, Carl, "said Bernie as she tossed the marker she'd used to him.

"There isn't any link at all between Carl and King, so the common denominator has to be the other two, or at least one of them," said Sharon. "You didn't know who Tucker was before that day in court, so it has to be the DA, Reece."

Carl could feel all of their eyes on him. He would have liked to say, "Oh yeah, I remember now, I saw Tucker give the DA a bribe while King watched." All he could really say was other than seeing him in the courthouse hallway occasionally, he didn't know Reece from Adam.

"Are you saying we have been spinning our

wheels trying to find out more about Wiley Tucker when we should have been looking at the DA?" asked Meyer.

Bernie nodded her head slowly. "We have nowhere else to go. Somehow those three are tied together. Until we find out how, we're lost."

Mike, leaning against the edge of Meyer's desk, stopped chewing. He studied the paper for a second and then said, "We do know whatever it is, it happened a year or more ago. The only people we know who had contact with them then were Collins and Wise. Tomorrow morning, we find out what those two can remember."

"If Alonzo King is gone, how can we find out about him?" asked Sharon.

Bernie folded her arms and considered the question. "If I had some help, we could search in the computer and the unentered files at the department. It's boring and dirty, but we might find something about Mr. King in the files more current than the ones I have downstairs. We would have to do it when the brass are gone for the day. I would be hard-pressed to explain having a civilian snooping around in there."

Maggie, already at Meyer's keyboard, searched the Internet for Alonzo King's life.

"Carl, I think if we are going to find out anything about this man, we're going to have to find someone who actually knew him–family, friends, whoever. They have to be out there somewhere," said Meyer as he slapped the armrests of his wheelchair. It was obvious he realized he couldn't get out to help find these people and it frustrated him.

"I wouldn't know where to start looking, unless Mom comes up with something."

Mike raised his hand as if he wanted permission to speak. "His body had to go somewhere. Maybe I can find out who claimed it. If there was a funeral, someone had to pay for it."

"That's where you go, Carl. If his body was found by someone from Mount Zion, and he was a deacon there, maybe they can help you find his family," said Meyer.

Carl waited to ask Sharon if she wanted to ride along with him to Mount Zion. He heard Sharon and Bernie making plans to meet at the door of the parking ramp for the sheriff's department at six. He was listened to his non-date slip away. It bothered him more than he cared to admit.

Slightly miffed, he told Meyer he was headed to Mount Zion and slipped out with only Mike and Meyer noticing.

As Carl paid the extra five dollars to liberate his suit from Dale's, he considered sending a bill for the dry cleaning to his mom. Getting into the SUV, he realized that just hours ago he was trying to think of a way to get out of the same date he was now free of. He mumbled to himself as he merged onto the expressway, "Too old to date, anyhow."

In spite of urban sprawl, Mount Zion was still a bit out in the country. Carl turned at the sign listing the hours of services, onto a gravel drive. Tall junipers lined the shoulders and appeared to be reaching to heaven. It was much cooler here than out on the highway, and it struck Carl how relaxing and peaceful it was.

Driving up to a hand-lettered sign pointing to EXTRA PARKING, Carl followed its arrow. Passing through a gap in the trees, he entered a large field partially filled with cars. At the far end was a circus-type tent, with a white flag bearing a blue cross flying from one of its poles.

The pulse of a bass guitar was working its way through the windows of the SUV as it drew closer to the tent. Carl parked a discreet distance away from the other vehicles. He looked back at his truck as he strolled toward the tent. He had no justification for parking all alone, at least two hundred feet from the nearest car. It troubled him and he didn't know why.

A huge choir was singing a spiritual to which Carl knew some of the words and melody. He determined it would be better to come back another time; he certainly didn't want to get involved with or interrupt the service. As he turned to leave, he bumped into a huge man in a three-piece suit who smiled and asked, "May I be of help, young man?"

"I don't want to interrupt the service. I can come back later."

"This meeting is going to last three days; can you wait that long for what you need? Let's step back a ways so we don't have to shout so."

They were a good two hundred feet from the tent when Carl realized they were headed toward a huge church. He had missed seeing it over his shoulder as he drove between the trees.

A large covered patio on the side of the building provided shade for about forty tables covered with white cloths.

The man motioned Carl to a chair but remained standing. He extended his right hand to Carl and said, "Welcome. I'm Reverend Charles Thompson, pastor here at Mount Zion. And you are…?"

"Carl Fletcher, sir," said Carl as he rose to shake the hand of the man whose smile seemed to make the air around him glow.

"I do hope you haven't come to complain about the noise. We've had a company come and take decibel readings at the end of the drive. They assure us the noise levels are acceptable."

"I don't know anything about that, sir."

"A few people see fit to complain about our meeting every year. It seems to be their mission in life. I apologize for mistaking you for one of them. What is it you have come for? I may be wrong again, but I doubt it's for the revival."

"No sir. I came about a gentleman who belonged to your church. Alonzo King."

As Carl said the name, the big man bowed his head to say softly, "Please care for him, Lord.

"Brother King was faithful to the Lord Jesus and all of God's children. When the Lord took him home, it was a loss to us all at Mount Zion."

"Did he have any family here at the church?"

"Alonzo treated everyone he met as his own. In the sense you mean, he had no blood relations anywhere."

"Are you sure, sir? It would be most helpful if I could speak to someone close to him. Who claimed his body? Who buried him?"

Crossing the Centerline

"I claimed his body, son. His brothers and sisters in the faith laid his earthly body to rest. His grave is beyond that row of trees, just past the tent. I am quite positive about his lack of relatives. Mount Zion has an extensive genealogy department. We are able to trace the families of most of our members to when their predecessors were brought to this continent. As for meeting someone who was close to Brother King, we can help, if first you might tell me why."

"Reverend Thompson, I'm willing to tell you why if you'll promise me it'll remain confidential. It may be a matter of life and death."

"My word, on my soul to God. What is troubling you so?"

A lady wearing a flowered dress and a huge picture hat approached the table with a tray. She set it down; without conversation, she moved back to those gathered at the far end of the patio.

The pastor made a motion toward the pitcher she had brought. Carl acknowledged it with a nod and poured lemonade into the two glasses. The large man unbuttoned his vest while Carl sipped and decided where to begin.

"Some friends and I believe Mr. King's death was not an accident."

"The coroner declared it was. Why would you and your friends think differently?"

"Because we think the same person we believe killed him has attempted to kill me more than once."

"Who are these 'we' that believe you are in this peril?"

"Some of them were actually there when there

was an attempt to kill me. It put them in danger also. One of the people was my mother."

"When you said you thought Alonzo was killed. I assumed, falsely it seems, it was racially motivated. I have to apologize for a bit of stereotypical thinking. Perhaps you can tell me how you think this person has selected you and Brother Alonzo as victims? I don't know you at all; I've known Mr. King for some time. It's early yet, but I truly don't see a commonality."

"We both had occasion to come in contact with this individual. I learned something by accident he wanted kept secret. Mr. King was involved in a scuffle at a local bar with the same man."

"That would be the drunk who tried to run Alonzo out of Ziggy's. He told me about the incident. At first I thought it was racial, but Alonzo assured me it was not. He said it was about a project he was involved in that would soon be completed. It was something he intended to surprise us with here at Mount Zion. We never found out what it was, of course, with the house burning down before we could take possession of the property."

"You were supposed to take possession of Alonzo King's house?"

"Yes. Many of our members who wish to gift some or all of their possessions to the church leave a copy of their wills right here. We can then follow through with the probate procedure. Unfortunately, Alonzo's home burned just days after his passing."

"Did you see to the demolition of the remains of the house?"

Crossing the Centerline

"No, the district attorney came by a few days after the fire and told me it was a safety hazard and had to be cleaned up. He said he would have a highway crew working in the area take care of it. I went to take pictures of it the next day. By that time everything but the basement had been removed."

"You said you could put me in touch with someone who knew him well. Would it be possible today?"

"Almost any time at all. I'm sure Brother Gilliam would love to have your company. I must get back to the meeting for a time. It will take about forty-five minutes, then I can meet you right here. You can come down to the tent if you wish. There's no obligation on your part when they pass the plate." A wide grin crossed the preacher's face. "If you'd rather, you can wait right here. Enjoy the shade and lemonade. I'll be praying on what you told me while I'm inside."

Carl stayed on the patio for a time, sipping lemonade. Finally, curiosity got the better of him. He wandered to the edge of the parking lot to hear the music.

The lemonade lady came up behind him unnoticed, placed her hand on his arm, and led him into the tent. "Come along, young man. There's no need to stand here in this heat. No one is going to hurt you inside. We'll find you a chair here in the back."

It was nearly five-thirty before the preacher came down the aisle to gather up Carl. "I have a few moments now. I can introduce you to Brother

Gilliam. He was closer to Alonzo than anyone. They were deacons together when Alonzo died–or should I say, was murdered."

Carl surmised it was the reverend's way of letting him know he had accepted his explanation.

Carl had a few stereotypical thoughts of his own and was expecting the preacher to drive a conservative sedan. Instead, Reverend Thompson led him to a bright red jeep with the top removed. "Hope you don't mind the car? I got used to these when I was in Vietnam. I've had one in my life ever since. I think it helps to remind me of what I used to be, and that's not always a bad thing."

The reverend made a hard left, heading across a large field, not coming in contact with the driveway again until they reached a parking lot. They pulled up in front of a red brick ranch-style building trimmed in white. It was much like the home Carl grew up in.

The preacher read the look on Carl's face. "I'm sorry, I should have explained–it's Carl, right? Isaiah Gilliam is a resident of our retirement and care center. A good number of our congregation never had the type of job that would have gained a pension. About two years after we came here, my wife Delphinia started to work toward creating a facility to help our elders maintain a life of dignity."

They parked near a patio similar to the one on the side of the church. As the large man exited the jeep with a nimbleness Carl and his brace couldn't achieve, a number of the residents waved and shouted greetings.

Carl trailed behind as the reverend

enthusiastically greeted everyone in his path. Carl was reminded of a politician glad-handing his constituents, and immediately felt guilty for the thought. The notion that this guy was too good to be true lingered in his mind.

"I hope all of you will come over on the bus to the meeting later, when it's cooler. I'm saving seats down front for all of you," the reverend called out as he and Carl passed through the double doors into the building.

"Brother Gilliam stays inside on these warm humid days; his respiratory function isn't all we want it to be."

Reverend Thompson tapped gently on one of the doors lining a long hallway.

"Don't be out there a-tappin', come on in with ya," came a masculine voice from behind the door. "Reverend, you come for a whuppin' at cribbage, or is that a new victim you brung me?"

"Brother Gilliam, I have some unpleasant news for you. This young man came seeking your help to solve a mystery. He has convinced me our Brother King's fall which took him from us was not an accident. He believes someone intentionally killed our friend."

Tears formed in the old man's eyes; Carl felt he could see a lot of life leaving Isaiah's body. "They still doing that stuff out there? When it goin' to end, Reverend, when?"

"It's not what you think, Isaiah; the same people are trying to kill this boy here, too. We have to help him find out who it is before anyone else suffers. I want you to promise me as a friend you'll do everything you can to help him. I believe he was sent here for a purpose, and you are part of it."

"I do what you tell me, Reverend, I takes your word."

"Bless you, Isaiah. I'm sure Alonzo is smiling down on you right now. Carl, I'll be back for you in about an hour. If you must leave before then, tell the sisters down the hall; they will get you back to your car. I hope you find what you need. You and I will pray for this boy when I come back, Isaiah, and don't you forget it."

Carl found a chair in the corner and moved it near the one the old man sat in.

"What ya want from me, boy?" asked the old man as the reverend shut the door behind him.

"I'm sorry you lost your friend. I hoped you could give me some kind of idea why someone would want him dead; it's that simple." Carl regretted his choice of words as soon as they left his mouth. They hurt the old man. He could see it.

"There's nothing simple 'bout dyin', son. The only thing worse is killin'. Lonzo was the finest man I ever knew in all my days. Only time he harmed a soul was in the war. He saved my miserable life more than once, don't ya know."

"You were in the war with Mr. King?"

"Ya don't hafta call him Mr. King. He would have liked you to call him Lonzo. That's when we met, back then. He explained things to me, 'cause I never learned readin'. He took care of this old boy. Was you in the war, son?"

"No, sir, I never was."

"Then how'd you get that nasty limp of your leg there?"

"One of the men who I think killed Lonzo tried to kill me by running over my car with a big truck."

"You're lucky, boy; you could'a died then. I see in your eyes that ain't all, is it?"

"No, it's not. A young lady I wanted to marry died there."

"That's sad, my boy, real sad. You ain't just lookin' to get even, are ya? That'll eat your insides, boy. It will sour you up forever, that kinda hate."

"Right now I'm just trying to stay alive. They're still trying to get me, but I'm not sure why."

"I don't know why they would be trying to kill Lonzo neither. He was nothing but good to folks. All he cared about was helping folks. He spent most his time working on his house and garden over there."

"Reverend Thompson said he was working on some kind of surprise for the church. Do you happen to know what it was?"

"Now if he had told me, then it wouldn't'a been a surprise, would it?" said the old man in much the same tone which Nina took with Carl. "I has ta get on to the meeting. You can ride over on the bus if you want. I don't think I can be much help to ya, but come back again if you want."

"I just may do that, sir, if you don't mind."

A nurse came in to get Isaiah ready for the bus. Rather than bother anybody, Carl walked back toward the church. He decided he really liked this part of the world that until today was unknown to him. Arriving at the church patio, he stopped to thank the lemonade lady for her kindness.

"I'm glad you enjoyed the music. I hope my husband was able to help you. Come back whenever you wish. He says you are always welcome here."

"You must be Delphinia. I wanted to tell you how much I admire what you have done here."

"You mean what God has done here. I am just his hands. Come again, please."

Driving through the rows of trees back out onto the country road, Carl was at a loss which way to turn. He had nowhere in particular to be or anything to do. He wandered for a while, then for no real reason he drove through the construction on Highway 83. It was almost six on Saturday; there were no workers to be seen. The parking lot at Ziggy's was nearly full when he passed.

He was sick of the whole affair and toying with the idea of turning back to find Tucker so he could put an end to it. Yet he held back. Too many people had put in a lot of effort and risk to resolve this the right way to give up now.

Turning at the corner of Highway 83 and Council, Carl pulled the SUV over in front of what was left of Alonzo King's home. He tried to picture a manicured lawn and well-kept garden. There was nothing but tractor tire marks now. How strange the rain and snow hadn't washed them away, like someone had washed away Alonzo's life.

Shuffling around things he had accumulated in the back of the SUV, Carl found the new digital camera he had bought to take to Florida and forgotten about. It seemed silly even as he was doing it, but he took several pictures of the basement from a number of angles. It suddenly seemed necessary. Someone should make a record of what was important to Alonzo King. Maggie could print them out so he could show them to Isaiah. He was sure Alonzo's old friend would want one or two as a reminder of his old friend's place.

Carl felt better as he climbed back into the SUV. He wished he could go home to his boat, but for now he had no home. Then he remembered Meyer was landlocked in his loft. He thought it best to get back to see if Meyer needed anything.

Carl had underestimated Chuck and Hank by a long shot. While Carl was gone, they had rigged an electric boat winch so Meyer could lift himself out of bed. A refrigerator now sat next to the bed and the paper had been removed from the TV. All was again right with Meyer's little world.

"You had anything to eat, son? You've been gone all day."

"No, wasn't hungry."

"The old bat from next door stocked the fridge. Get yourself something and tell me what you found out at the church. Oh, you better call your mother first; she has been trying to reach you all day. Don't you ever turn that cell phone of yours on?"

"Battery is probably dead. No one ever called until two weeks ago. I don't really know why I had a phone before then."

Carl tried the desk phone. Maggie's line was

busy so he explored the sandwiches and soda in the refrigerator.

"Talked to an old friend of King's, says he was the salt of the earth. The man never did anything that wasn't good all his life, can't possibly figure why someone would want him dead."

"What's in the case?"

"Camera. I stopped and took some pictures of King's basement. It's all that's left of his place."

"If that's a chip camera, throw it into the PC right there. We can take a look."

"I don't know crap about those things. I was going to take the thing to the shop where I bought it to have them do the printing."

"That kind of defeats the purpose of a digital camera, doesn't it? Your mother taught me how to do this the other day."

"Mom is sure one busy lady."

Meyer ignored the remark and reached for the camera. He slid the chip out, then directed Carl to where it went into the computer. A few clicks of the wireless mouse, then the TV remote, and the big screen filled with one of Carl's artistic endeavors.

"It looks like it was a really big house, judging by the size of the basement," said Meyer.

"I hadn't really thought about it. I guess it was really something."

Meyer clicked from picture to picture. "What do you suppose he had all those doors in that wall for?"

"Don't know," said Carl between sandwich bites. "I didn't climb down there. Maybe they are root cellars or something like it. I was going to get some prints made for his friend at Mount Zion. I'll ask him about the doors when I take them over."

The phone rang. Meyer answered it, then tossed it to Carl while mouthing *Mom*.

Carl knew from Meyer's expression this wasn't going to be a friendly howdy. "Hey, Mom, what's up? How was I supposed to know? I heard her say she was meeting Bernie downtown to search for files. How long before he gets here? Okay, I'll change my shirt and be ready." He turned off the phone. "It would seem, Meyer, I'm not supposed to be here, but at the sheriffs department, only I don't remember anyone telling me. Now an armed escort is on its way to take me into custody and deliver me there."

"I expected as much. Sharon was under the impression you would be spending your day with her, scanning files. When they were here at lunchtime, she, quote, turned around and you were gone, end quote."

"I thought the date thing was off."

"That apparently leaves you as the *only* one with that thought."

"Trouble?"

"Deep."

"It wasn't really a date. It was more like a dinner away from her place."

"You are also the only one to have *that* thought."

"Deep trouble?"

"HUGE."

A short burp of a police car siren sounded below and Carl headed on his way.

Allan E. Ansorge

CHAPTER TWENTY
All Work and No Play

Carl told Mike of his day's activities on their way downtown. They had both discovered the same information about Alonzo King's death and burial. Carl didn't go into any particulars of his afternoon at Mount Zion or his intention to return there.

Mike parked in the underground ramp so his car would be less obvious. They used the stairs to gain entry to the first floor file storage area. Bernie and Sharon were not where the men expected them to be.

"Well, Carl, if you were a file clerk and you were here to review files, my guess would be you would do it in the file room. Obviously I'm wrong about that. You got any suggestions?"

"I'm not having a lot of luck following the female thought process right now. I don't think I'm the one you should ask."

"Carl, you stay here. No, better yet, go to the lunchroom. Buy yourself some coffee and try to look like you belong there. When I find the girls, I'll come and get you."

They went their separate ways, Carl down the hall to his left, Mike up another flight of stairs. Carl was at least thirty feet from the lunchroom door when he heard laughter coming from inside. He peeked around the doorjamb to see Sharon and Bernie seated at a long table piled two feet deep with file folders. Dale the janitor was at one end and another janitor sat at the other.

Bernie spotted him and waved him in. "Come on over, Carl. I want you to meet the new part-time girl they hired to help me get caught up. Now I won't have to work so many hours. This is Sharon. Sharon, Carl. He's rehabbing from injury, but should be back in the saddle soon, right, Carl?"

"Oh, right," said Carl, "any day now."

Sharon, sitting across the table from Carl, promptly kicked him in the shin. "I'm glad you're doing well, Carl," said Sharon through a forced smile. "I worry so about you boys; it seemed you were off forever."

Carl felt the shoe whiz past his leg again and decided to retreat to the candy machine.

"You want us to start carrying these back to the cabinets, Bernie?" asked Dale.

"If you could, it would be great, Dale. Just set them on the floor. I'll get them in the right places. Thank you so much, guys, you two are great."

Dale and the other janitor loaded the folders onto a freight cart and headed down the hall. Mike passed them in the hall as they attempted a high-speed corner. Not unlike Carl, he followed the laughter to the lunchroom to find his cohorts. They were drinking sodas and making a great deal more noise than he was comfortable with.

"Keep it down, will you? Do you want the whole building to know you're here?"

"They already do, Mike," said Bernie. "Who do you think helped us find all the files we wanted to see? The watch commander helped carry them in here. He's going to see what he can do about getting me more help so I don't have to come in on my own time to keep up."

"You were supposed to sneak in here and sneak out. What happened to that plan?"

"Relax, Mike. Why sneak when you can dance? It was all in vain anyway, all we got was tired eyes. I can just feel there is something we're missing in this deal, but I can't figure out what or where it is."

"Well, if your work is done here, let's get out before the powers that be decide to give you and me a permanent vacation."

"I have to get this stuff back in the drawers. You can give me a hand; we'll meet the others later."

"I'll fix something at the diner. Call when you leave here, and it'll be ready when you get there," said Sharon. "Come on, wanderer, I'll drive. I wouldn't want you to get lost again."

Carl waited until they were in the parking ramp to say, "I wasn't wandering. I went to church."

"I know. Meyer told me right after you left. This isn't exactly how I expected tonight to turn out. I was worried about you, you know. You shouldn't be out and about with Tucker waiting to pounce on you."

"I don't think he's likely to show up at a revival meeting any time soon, but then I never thought I would, either."

"Hop in, my prodigal son. I'll fix you a cup of coffee and you can tell me how sorry you are you stood me up."

"I didn't stand you up."

"'Cause it wasn't like a real date? Yeah, I heard

that. Maybe it wasn't like a real date because you didn't want it to be."

"Are you sure you wanted it to be?"

"I asked you, didn't I? But I won't again; it's too hard on both of us."

"Then I'll ask you."

Sharon slammed on the brakes as they passed the boat yard. "That damned old fool."

Meyer saw her car and tried to make it back into the building, but he couldn't get his chair to roll over the doorsill fast enough. Sharon was on him in a flash.

"Dropped a pencil out the window, came down to find it," Meyer insisted.

Her hands eased the chair over the bump. "Those windows don't open," was all she said as she pushed the chair onto the freight elevator. Without warning, she spun the chair around, pushing it out to the walkway and over to the diner. She tossed Carl the keys so he could handle the door. When the chair cleared the entrance, she gave it one hard shove into the room and ran to the kitchen.

Meyer looked over his shoulder at Carl. "Trouble?"

"*Huge.*"

Carl quietly went through the swinging doors. Sharon had put on an apron, more out of habit than necessity, and was standing at the stove. Carl worked his way around the stovetop island. When he was in front of her, he could see the tears on her cheeks.

"Can I help? I don't mean with cooking. I'm not worth much at it, but with anything else?"

"I don't think so. I doubt you can beat sense into him at his age."

"If you don't mind my saying so, you underestimate him. He's far from frail, and at his age he doesn't need a mother, you know."

"I worry."

"He's fine and getting better every day. Can I ask you something?"

"Go ahead."

"How did you two ever get together? Who is Meyer?"

"Let's just say he was a gift someone shared with me and leave it there for right now, okay? You've seen enough tears for today. Now get out of my kitchen. Go out there and keep an eye on the old bugger."

Meyer tried to read Carl's face as he returned from the kitchen. "Is she calming down any?"

"She's getting over it. I don't know why, but she worries about you."

"I used to think it was my good looks, now I think it's my wealth," said Meyer, with a grin toward the kitchen.

Sharon burst through the swinging doors with a cordless phone in her hand. She pushed the speaker button so they all could hear. "Go ahead, Maggie, we're all here."

"Carl, a man just tried to have me buzz him in. He said he was an old friend of yours. He wanted to come in to wait for you. I told him my son lives in San Diego. I don't know if he bought it. I'm not sure if he has left or not. Don't come near the place, do you hear me, Carl?"

"I hear you, Mom. Just stay inside. Leave the phone line open until I say to hang up. Make sure your door is deadbolted. Move some furniture in front of it, too. Get your gun out, but for God's sake don't use it until you are positive who's at the door, okay?"

"Gotcha, son."

Meyer had worked his way over to the door. He unlocked it and gave a short blast into the night with a hand-held air horn. Sharon stepped behind the counter to pull a nine-millimeter automatic with an extra loaded clip from a drawer. She handed it to Carl, who accepted it without question. He was headed to the door when Hank came in carrying a short-barrel pump shotgun.

"Patience, Carl," said Meyer. "Hank, I want you to go to Maggie's place, low profile from the back side. Carl is going to bring her out and you're all to get back here without being followed. We don't know how many people are over there or where. If there is only one bring him with you. We might want to chat with him. More than one, take a pass. Clear?"

"Clear."

"Carl, you have the hard part. For this to work, you have to be the bait. Hide the gun; don't show it unless you have to. Walk right up into the front entrance, go straight to Maggie's, bring her right out the front with you. Hank will have your six, don't do anything else. When you leave there, Hank will be behind you. You bring Maggie straight here. Is this clear to you?"

"Clear, but...."

"No buts, son, just do exactly as I said, no more, no less. You might want to try keeping your mother from spraying the place with lead, if you can. We'll keep Maggie on the telephone. You call my cell here when you are inside her building, then we can tell Maggie when to open the door. Clear?"

"Clear."

Hank and Carl headed to their cars at the boat shed as fast as Carl could.

"Hank, that isn't the same gun Chuck had the other day, is it?"

"No, I keep this one for formal occasions. Hurry up, Meyer wants this done now."

They left in separate vehicles, Carl wondering how they would explain the loaded guns if they got stopped for speeding.

Back in the diner, Meyer continued making plans. "Sharon, find Mike with your cell, then you stay on the line with Maggie while I fill him in. Maggie, Meyer here," he said into the phone. "You all right so far?"

"Fine, Meyer, and how are you doing?"

"Great. I'm sure you heard the plan. You have any questions?"

"Just one. How will I know when Carl is at the main entrance so I can buzz him in?"

"He'll call you on the intercom just like always. I think you better calm down a little, girl."

"Then you were serious about him walking right up through the main entrance. Are you crazy, Meyer? There could be someone out there waiting to shoot him or something! I have food here; I could have just waited them out."

"I know, dear lady, but this way we may have a chance to collect one of them. Here, Sharon wants a word. Be strong. I'll be right here if you need me. Remember, don't hang up."

Sharon and Meyer swapped phones. Meyer filled Mike in on the situation. Mike wanted Meyer to hold off so he could go to Fern Hill with a backup unit. He thought if they could get an arrest there, it would become a real case. Meyer convinced him that Maggie's safety was more important than anything else and it was time to get her out of there. Meyer reminded him they weren't certain there was anyone still at Maggie's and Mike could come off as the boy who cried wolf.

Mike turned his car around, heading toward Fern Hill. He knew he was too far away to be of help unless Carl and Hank trapped someone of interest.

Hank had disappeared in traffic by the time they had driven two blocks. Carl wondered how Hank knew where his mother lived, but he was learning not to question these things anymore. Sometimes it was better just to accept and move on.

There was no sign of Hank as Carl pulled into the circle drive at Fern Hill. He left the SUV in the no-parking area near the front door. When two elderly ladies, seated on a bench at the entrance, glanced from him to the No Parking sign to show their disapproval, he felt he needed to explain. As he leaned on the buzzer he said to them, "Mom's old arthritis is acting up, gonna run her over to the doc's."

Blue dress turned to flowered dress and said, "He's such a nice boy."

The lock in the door clicked, and the two ladies went through the door with Carl. Suppose they were part of it, Carl thought. He managed to position himself behind them, just in case. What were they doing out at this time of night? He wasn't going anywhere until they went somewhere.

Where they were going was to tell the security guard some weirdo was in the building who claimed to be taking his mother to the doctor at eight at night.

Carl passed up the elevator and made the stairs in record time. He didn't see three men leave the car parked across the street. Two of them waited at the front door for someone to answer one of the several buzzers they had pushed. They hoped to get into the building before their quarry got too far away. The third member of the group had made his way to the rear entrance when he suddenly felt the barrel of a sawed off shotgun in the small of his back, prompting him to say, "What the hell are you doing?"

"The important thing is, I know what you're doing," said Hank as he pulled a handgun from the man's waistband. He whispered in the man's ear he wanted complete silence and nothing less, while steering him toward the other two at the entrance. "Hang on there, fellas, I can get you in," he said from the shadow of the larger man.

They didn't grasp the situation until Hank was on top of them. He ordered them back to their car three-wide so he could watch them all. They were either smart or scared enough; they didn't try a movie-type move. When they reached the far side of their car, Hank relieved them of three guns and two long-blade knives. He had them casually leaning against their car when Carl and Maggie came out of the building, with two suitcases, and left in the SUV. Hank used one of the knives to bore a hole in each of the right-side tires of the car.

"It's your lucky day, boys; my boss told me to try not to kill you." Then Hank disappeared back into the shrubs along the side of the building.

Just as they heard a squeal of tires from behind the building, a sheriff's squad car pulled up and Mike McCaffery climbed out of it. "Looks like you have a problem here, gentlemen. Anything I can do to help?"

Back at the diner, Mike expressed regret he didn't have anything to hold the three of them on. "I couldn't even be sure the IDs they'd given us were real. Now if I had caught them in possession of an unregistered firearm..." Mike looked pointedly down at the weapons Hank had placed on the counter.

"The one thing we are sure of is that they are not pros. These are target and hunting guns. We can have Hank look at the road crew pictures to see if any of the three of them came from there," said Meyer.

Sharon had an arm around Maggie's shoulder. "Maggie, I think it would be best if you stayed here with me where the boys can look out for us. I think it would be safer than somewhere in a motel. What do you say?"

"Thank you, Sharon. I accept...under the condition you find me some way to help out around here. I don't want to be a leech."

"Consider it done," said Sharon.

"Where is Bernie?" asked Carl.

"I called her down to Fern Hill to have her follow those yahoos when I turned them loose. They already know what you, Hank, and I look like. She was the likely candidate," Mike explained.

"Do you think it's safe?" asked Sharon.

"She'll be fine. The department has already used her on stings and stakeouts. She knows what she's doing. I'm heading out to get some rest. I'll be back by six in the morning to meet with Will Wise. See you all later."

As Carl pushed Meyer in the wheelchair back to the loft, Meyer had him stop at the corner of the building, where Sharon had caught him before, looking at the stars. "It's great to be alive, ain't it, kid?"

"You bet, Jim. It gets better every day," said Carl as he playfully bumped the side of Meyer's chair.

CHAPTER TWENTY-ONE
Well, What Do You Know?

The diner parking lot was empty except for Chuck's van as Carl pushed Meyer up the ramp to the front door early the next morning. Carl asked Shirley if his mother was down yet.

"Down? Hell, she's done two days' worth of work already. Not all of us can sleep in like the wealthy, you know."

"And where would she be doing this work?"

Shirley waved a hand toward the kitchen.

Meyer looked at Carl. "I see your stock with the pink dress ladies is soaring. How do you do it?"

Carl found Maggie in the kitchen dressed in one of the pink uniforms and a nearly floor-length red rubber apron, Carl didn't recognize Maggie at first. He didn't think it possible, but it appeared she was doing dishes.

"Morning, Carl. Hey, come and look at this machine. It will do over five hundred dishes an hour. I have to get one of these."

"Mom, you've cooked your whole year's limit in the last three weeks. You would never use something like this."

"I might if I had company. It could come in handy."

"Collins and Wise are on their way, if you want to meet with them."

"Be right out," she called as she grabbed a stack

of sterilized plates with her big rubber gloves and put them into an overhead rack.

Rick Collins and Will Wise walked through the diner door at exactly six-thirty. Will was somewhat taken aback by the committee of six waiting for him. Carl did the introductions and explained that breakfast was on him. Rick and Will ordered from Nina; she made her way to the kitchen mumbling about more non-tippers.

"Will, I guess Rick sort of filled you in on what we're dealing with here. The situation has tightened up a bit since we saw you, Rick. Last night, three guys showed up at Maggie's looking for Carl. We had sort of prepared for the worst and managed to wet-blanket their plan. I might add they were armed, but didn't appear to be pros," said Mike.

"What did you charge them with?" asked Rick.

"Well, nothing, actually. We felt at the time it was best we try to tail them. We wanted to see if we could connect them with the person who sent them. Unfortunately, they went their separate ways by cab and we lost them. A fellow helped us pick two of them out of photos of the road crew on the Highway 83 project. We can find those two when we need them. It appears they used their own IDs, so we have a good handle on them."

"What is it you want from me?" asked Will.

"We know the arrest report you filled out about the deal at Ziggy's was dumped and a revised version put in its place. Do you have any idea why that would have been done and by whom?"

"First, you answer a question for me. Why didn't

you hang on to these three jokers when you had them? You could have used whatever means necessary to find out what they knew then."

"Fair question. Let's just say that the person who, at great personal risk, disarmed these people on Maggie's behalf was not officially authorized to do so," said Mike. He glanced over Rick's shoulder at Hank, who was nursing a cup of coffee just outside the door of the little meeting room.

"You've hired your own gun?"

"Not quite. We borrowed the expertise behind the gun. We needed help right away and he volunteered. It was a matter of self-defense," said Carl.

"I'm proud of you people," said Will Wise. "You're finishing something that was brushed under the rug a long time ago. As far as I've been told, you have a copy of the second report, correct? Rick has brought you a copy of the original with my sworn affidavit that is identical to the one I filled out the night of the arrest. Now to answer your question…who?

"I had turned the original report over to Inspector Nelson. I worked with him for a lot of years. He had his faults, but he would never fix evidence. It had to be someone who had access to it after him. Nelson retired about four months before me. My guess is whoever changed it waited until he was gone. They knew if Nelson found out, it would hit the fan. By then, all the paperwork would be at the prosecutor's office. Stands to reason that's where it got changed. It's a guess, but a damn good one."

Bernie leaped from her chair. "I knew it! I knew it from the start, it's James Reece."

"I don't get the connection. Why would a DA want to put a hit out on a deputy? What did you do to him?" asked Will.

"We're guessing here, but I saw a piece of paper by mistake that threw the case out against your buddy, Wiley Tucker. We think he was afraid I found out he changed your report so he could justify dismissing the charges."

"That was a long time ago. Why go after you now?"

"It had me wondering, too. It probably all comes down to timing. I spent the better part of a year in and out of hospitals. I never returned to the department, so Reece felt safe. James Reece recently got elected to fill a vacant seat in the state senate. Maybe he thought I might be a problem for his campaign. If he figures he has bigger fish to fry, like governor, I still could be a problem. At least he may think so."

Will pushed his chair from the table. "I'll be in town until Wednesday. If you want me, you can reach me through Rick. I never thought I was important enough to be available twenty-four/seven so I don't have a cell phone. I wish you all luck finding out who's making your lives miserable."

Rick and Will's departures left the group of six at a loss. They had expected more than what they had learned.

"I believe the ball is in your court, ladies. Bernie, you have to find out if this case-dropping was a habit of the DA's. Maggie, when someone runs for office, their life gets looked at pretty closely. You look into the life of the new senator. Get to know him better than his wife does," said Mike. "I'll start down at the station to see what rumors I can turn into truths. Meyer, since you are temporarily grounded, could you try to organize what we already know and what Bernie and Maggie find?

"Carl, this attempt at your mom's has me scared. I think it's time to listen to her and lay low for a while. I don't know how you can protect yourself if you are out and about when we don't know who is after you."

"Where would you like me to hide, Mike, under Meyer's sofa?"

"Funny, but not a bad idea. This business last night has changed everything. What if those people had decided to snatch Maggie as a hostage, or worse? You may not like it, but it's time to circle the wagons to be sure we protect our own."

"You're right, Mike. I'll do what you suggest. What is that, exactly?"

"Travel alone, but let Sharon know where you are going and what path you're taking. She can follow you at a distance, so if you need help, she can call for it without being noticed."

"Oh, right, no one will notice the fire-engine-red Jaguar."

Maggie moved around the table to slap the back of Carl's head. "Cut the sarcasm, honey, she can use my car. Just remember, if you hadn't stuck your nose into someone else's briefcase, we all wouldn't be spending our lives trying to save yours. I think it's high time you cut the woe-is-me act and thank your friends."

It was hard to tell who in the group was most uneasy with her outburst, but there was only one way to raise the pall falling over the room.

"You are right, Mom. I'm sorry. All of you, thank you."

The tension eased when Sharon put her hand on his shoulder and asked, "What are we up to, my leader, and where are we going?"

"I think it's time I went to church. I'll sketch you a map."

CHAPTER TWENTY-TWO
Words of Wisdom

As he neared Highway 83, Carl pulled off the county road into a convenience store parking lot. He waited until Sharon passed by in Maggie's Taurus, and just a bit longer, to make sure she wasn't being followed. She had parked in front of the big wooden doors of the church and was still in the car when he arrived.

"How did I get here before you? Did you stop somewhere? That's not part of the program," Sharon said as she walked to the open driver's side window of the SUV.

Carl didn't want to admit he was looking out after her, perhaps even to himself. With a shrug, he went for the graceful white lie. "I stopped at the store back there. I thought the SUV was making a noise."

"Right," said Sharon with a tone letting him know it was a bad story and she knew it.

"Hop in. The home is down the drive, past the church."

"What home? I thought this guy worked here."

"It's too long a story for right now, but a good one. I'll tell you later."

Carl found a place in the shade to park and left the windows down. Sharon reached through the open window to lock the door on her side.

"Come this way. I want you to meet the lady working in the flower bed."

Carl took Sharon by the arm and led her to Delphinia. "Excuse me, Mrs. Thompson, I don't know if you remember me…"

"Of course I do, Mr. Fletcher. Would you please call me Delphinia. And you are, young lady…?"

"Sharon Waters. It's a pleasure to meet you."

"I'm sure the pleasure is mine. If you are a friend of Mr. Fletcher, you are very welcome here. Can I get you two something?"

"No ma'am, we're fine, and it's Carl, if you wouldn't mind."

"Of course, Carl. Let me see if I can find Charles for you, he's around here somewhere."

"Actually, I came to see Isaiah. I brought him some photos I thought he might like to have. They are of what's left of Mr. King's home and land. Honestly, they are also my excuse to stop in and see him again."

"I expected you would be back. He has been telling me there are things you and he have in common. I'm sure one of them is a kind heart. He will be thrilled to see you and your lovely friend. He has an eye for a pretty girl, you know."

"Well then, we have that in common, at least."

"If you would do me the favor of coaxing him out onto the patio, I believe a little sun and fresh air would be good for him."

Carl smiled. "I don't think he would come out at my request, but we have someone here who might be able to lead him to the light, in a matter of speaking."

"You are a dear but sassy boy. I can see why you like him, my dear." She smiled at Sharon. "Come, let's roust the old boy out."

"Isaiah, it's Carl. We met a few days ago."

"Yes, yes, and who's that pretty thing behind ya there?"

"This is my friend Sharon. We were wondering if you have a few minutes to go out to the patio and chat?"

"We can talk here, can't we?"

"Mr. Gilliam, Carl here has a doctor who insists he get as much fresh air as possible, and it is lovely out," said Sharon.

"If you wants to get in the sun, young lady, that be fine with me. Give me a little push there, boy."

A compromise was reached between Sharon and Isaiah to sit under the roof of the patio. The three of them settled around a table. Shortly, Delphinia appeared with a pitcher of lemonade and three glasses.

"Why don't you sit with us a spell, Missus?"

"I have a few things to catch up on, Isaiah. Maybe I'll stop back by when I'm done."

Isaiah shook his head as Delphinia walked away. "She don't never get done; that lady is a working fool. Day or night she be on the go. Has you finished up the business we was talking about last time I seen ya?"

"No, and it's okay to talk about it, Sharon knows."

"Well, don't be troubling on it, little girl, he's a smart boy here. He'll work it all out fine."

"Isaiah, I brought you something. I don't know if

you'd call it a present, though. I thought you might want to have some pictures of Alonzo's place, at least what's left of it."

The old man fished in his shirt pocket to come up with a pair of glasses. "I never wore these till the dia-bee-tee caught up with me. My, my, they sure messed up the place, didn't they? Lonzo's house and his big garden all gone now. They left nothin'. Makes a man wonder what happen to all his things, his books and papers on the railroad and such. How that man collected stuff on the railroad."

"It's so sad. I hope the pictures don't upset you. They do me," said Sharon.

"I been around so long, little girl, I cried most of my tears away by now. It's kinda hard to figure why someone wanted Lonzo dead. I'll be turning ninety-one tomorrow; it sure would be nice if you two come for cake with me, 'bout noon. Okay?"

"We would love to. Maybe we can come up with a happier treat for your birthday," said Sharon as Carl nodded in agreement.

"You just bring your pretty smile, little gal, that's plenty for me. I see the preacher headed this way. I think he wants a word with ya. I'll see you at the party tomorrow." The chair turned on a dime and Isaiah rolled back to the door.

"Hello, Carl. I'm sorry to interrupt," said the reverend. "It looks like I spoiled your visit. I did want to ask a favor before you left. I wonder if you could tell me how I could get a copy of the coroner's report on Alonzo's death? All I ever received was a death certificate."

"May I ask why?" said Carl.

"You have created some doubts in my mind I have to put to rest. As they say, information is power."

"We have been invited for cake tomorrow. Let me see what I can do by then."

"You have access to something like that?"

"We know a guy who knows a guy."

"I don't want you to do anything illegal or get into any kind of trouble."

"Well, anyone can go through channels to get that type of thing. We have just learned how to expedite things," said Sharon.

"How do you do, I'm Charles Thompson, Reverend Thompson."

"Yes, I know, sir. Trust me, we would never do anything to harm you or even embarrass you. Never," said Sharon.

"I do trust you, young lady. Thank you for reminding me there are things involved here more important than the title *reverend*. I look forward to seeing you both tomorrow. Thank you again."

Carl grinned as he reached through the open window to unlock the SUV.

"I'm glad I got to be your shadow, Carl. You really meet some nice people at churches. I can see why you wanted to come back. You really like Isaiah, don't you?"

"There is a kind of truth or something in his attitude that strikes a chord with me. Don't know why."

"Maybe it's a birds-of-a-feather thing. Where else would you like to spend your day hiding out?"

"I think we should go to a store far away from here and shop for a picnic."

"What picnic?"

"The one I'm inviting you to right now."

"It would be very close to a date. I thought we had given up on that."

"No, *you* gave up. I haven't started yet. Would you like to go on a picnic date with me, right now Miss?" He marveled at how the words came so easily, without a hitch or a stutter.

"Yes, I really would, sir."

CHAPTER TWENTY-THREE
Curiosity All Around

Carl arrived at the diner about two minutes ahead of Sharon. Maggie, still in a pink uniform, was pouring coffee for Meyer.

"Tips good today, Mom?"

"I ain't going to tell you. You're the type who would turn his mother in to the IRS. Coffee?"

"Please."

"Were you at that church all day?"

"No."

"It's nearly five. You were supposed to check in with Meyer on occasion so we knew where you were."

"I'm sorry, time just slipped away. I'll do better from now on, I promise."

"It's okay, Carl," said Meyer. "Your mother worries, you know. Where is your watch dog?"

"I thought she was right behind me. There, she just drove in."

"Watch the look on her face. I have something to show her."

Sharon flew through the door, carrying grocery bags filled with the remains of the picnic. "You could have helped with this, Carl, you bought most of it." The bags nearly hit the floor when she realized Meyer was standing in front of the wheelchair. "Are you supposed to be doing that? You sit down before you hurt yourself!"

"It's okay, kid. Dr. Blackman put on this fiberglass walking cast this afternoon. I start therapy tomorrow and can stand a little at a time."

"Why didn't you tell me? I would have taken you."

"Chuck took a seat out of his van. We rolled the old chariot here right in. Don't fret so, girl, you'll make yourself sick. You have a good time at Mount Zion?"

"It was great. I met some really nice people there."

"You two must be starved. What can I get you?" asked Maggie.

"I'm fine, I had plenty at the picnic," said Carl.

"Reverend Thompson threw a picnic for you?" asked Meyer.

"No, Carl and I went on a picnic," Sharon explained.

Maggie couldn't resist. "What picnic? Where was it?"

"It was just a picnic, Mom. You know, food, blanket, ants. A picnic."

Bernie came through the door with her arms full of papers and files.

Carl wrapped an arm around Bernie's shoulder "Hey, Bernie, were you able to do the favor we asked for?"

"I have some of it here. Mike is supposed to pick up the rest on his way here."

"You're an absolute doll and I'll love you forever," said a smiling Carl.

"Well, you're entirely welcome. I promise to love

you forever too. You can start looking through this stuff if you want."

Maggie motioned Bernie out to the diner area and whispered, "They went on a picnic."

"At the church?"

"They won't say where, but it wasn't at the church. It was their picnic, just them and some ants."

"You mean a date-type picnic?"

"I guess so."

"Well, I'll be…"

Bernie sat down next to Sharon in the back room of the diner. "If any of these are what you need, we'll have to make copies. Most of them are originals. So, what kind of day did you have, tagging along behind my new life-long love over there?"

"Picnic."

Just as Bernie was about to press the point, Mike came through the door like a pass rusher on speed. "You guys will never believe what I've got."

"How about newfound wealth? I've always wanted to hang out with rich people," said Maggie.

"Right now it's better than money. In my business, it's called hard evidence. Here, there are copies for everyone, read and enjoy. I have to go to the bathroom."

Bernie waited for Mike outside the men's room door. "They went on a *picnic*."

"Who are 'they'?"

"Carl and Sharon."

"Nice. At the church?"

"Not at the church, we don't know where."

"Okay."

"Like, just the two of them, a *date* picnic."

"Okaaaay, that's even nicer. What does all of this mean?"

"I don't know, but we have to find out."

"Why?"

Bernie gave him a look capable of wilting weeds. She whispered, "Men!" under her breath, and joined the others.

"This lab report is a little over my head," said Meyer, "What does it mean in layman's terms?"

"Sharon, why don't you do the honors? I'm sure you can do better than I can," said Mike.

Sharon frowned at him, rattled the papers a bit to let him know snooping into her past was not appreciated and neither was the comment. "In a nutshell, this appears to be a preliminary coroner's report on the death of Alonzo King. On page seven it mentions a foreign substance appearing on the clothing and body of the victim. The substance was identified as human blood of a type other than the victim's."

"You're saying the coroner actually filed a report stating he thought King was murdered?" asked Maggie. "I didn't find anything like that in the newspaper files."

"You wouldn't. Coroners usually don't release information like that to the press. They have a self-imposed gag order in an effort to avoid contaminating a case before it's tried," said Sharon.

They all fell silent when Terry Jeffords, the Crime Scene Investigator, came into the diner's meeting room. "Hey, Mike, got what you wanted. It took a while to scan all the photos and print them. I also emailed them to the address you gave me, just in case. Where is that place? It didn't have a GOV suffix."

"It's not really important right now. You know Carl and Bernadette here. This is Meyer, in the chair, Sharon owns this place, and this is Carl's mom, Maggie."

Mike gave Maggie a quick glance, then one at the ceiling. She understood perfectly, excused herself, and made her way to the computer in Sharon's office to verify that the pictures had arrived in email.

Jeffords spread the photos out on a table and asked Mike exactly what he was looking for.

"I don't know, Terry, you tell me. What do you see here?"

"Well, I didn't do this scene. I started here after this. You said you had a copy of a written report. Can I take a look at it?"

Bernie passed Terry a copy. Sharon asked him if she could get him anything. Soon there was a coffee cup in his hand. "I don't see where any documentation was prepared for trial, so they never caught who did this."

"Terry, are you saying definitely murder?" asked Mike.

"Did you have doubts? You're kidding, right? You have massive trauma to the head, second-party blood on the victim, and, if you look at the pictures, there isn't enough blood on the floor to indicate he bled to death there. He was dead before he went down the steps. It's all right here in the report and pictures."

"The report doesn't say murder anywhere," said Meyer.

"They never really do. The coroner's job is to find and demonstrate cause of death. The investigators and prosecutors are supposed to combine their reports with ours to determine if there is a crime, then solve and prosecute it."

"Terry, this was never prosecuted. The DA's office said they had no suspects or motive. After about a week, it was filed as unsolved and never touched again," said Mike.

"Do you know which DA handled it?"

"Oh yes, but he's no longer in the area."

"It appears to me you have enough right here to hang him for suppression of evidence and malfeasance. What I'm not sure of is who you should go to with it. Sometimes it's hard to tell the good guys from the bad, I guess."

"If we go now, we can haul him out of the office he has now. Unless he is willing to cut a deal, we'll never find out who or why. If his career is already ruined, why should he cooperate? We would like to see if we can put together a few more pieces of the puzzle first."

"I don't know if I can go along with this. It seems you and I are obligated to report it to someone. I think we could really be in a jam if we don't."

"Terry, six minutes ago you didn't even know this existed. You can walk out the door right now and turn back the clock. There isn't anyone at this table who'll say you were ever here. The thing is, the DA, Reece, had to have a good reason to take this kind of risk. When we find out what he got out of it and from whom, we take the whole thing downtown to the state attorney general."

"I think I can answer part of it with what I found out this morning," said Maggie.

"I think I better get home, my supper's getting cold. Mike, let me know when I can climb out from under the rock where I'll be hiding." Terry Jeffords gave a small shake of his head waved to all and left the building.

"What do you have, Mom?"

"I got to thinking…how could a DA move from here up north and get elected in such a short period of time? No one up there had even heard of him six weeks before the election."

"So how did he?" asked Bernie.

"Total media saturation. Campaign finance laws require you to disclose where your money comes from and where you spend it. Senator Reece had an ad every half hour on all three local TV stations in his new district. He had twenty-five billboards for five weeks and a different full-page photo ad in two papers every day for three weeks. They had to have fudged the books. The TV time alone had to cost more than his reported total expenses."

"He didn't make that kind of money as a DA. Who footed the bill?" asked Meyer.

"He got a maximum corporate contribution from Tripplete LLC and another fifty thousand dollars personally from Vernon Tripplete. Then Tripplete's wife sweetened the pot with another fifty thousand."

"Who are the Tripplets? Why does that name sound familiar?" asked Sharon.

"It's on the side of all the equipment they are using to pave Highway 83. You drove past it yesterday," said Carl.

"There is one bit of news," said Maggie. "The Tripplettes don't live in Manitowoc County. Their name doesn't show up on the property tax rolls either."

"They must really like Reece, or they had a strong interest in making sure Wiley Tucker was taken care of. How did you find all of this out, Mom?"

"Good detective work, son. That, plus I owe an exclusive to a secretary who wants to be a reporter at the Manitowoc Herald."

Meyer shifted in his chair and cleared his throat. "After all of this, we are going to have to come up with a new plan. Carl, you are grounded. You spend the next few days working in my shop. Consider it rent. Our neighborhood vandal did a number on Anderson's boat and we could use the help." He was speaking to Carl but it was obvious he was looking at Maggie. "Mike, you asked this Jeffords fellow for time. Did you have any idea what we were going to do with it to put an end to this mess?"

Mike rubbed his chin. "First, I would like to know whose blood was on Alonzo King's body. There is no guarantee it was the killer's, but a jury might see it that way. I'm betting it was either Wiley

Tucker's or Symons' blood. Then we have to figure out why this Vernon Tripplete wanted King dead."

"The only way you would be able to prove the blood came from either of those two would be to get a DNA scan of all three of them. I don't see our pal Wiley submitting a sample out of the goodness of his heart. The other two are long gone, not much hope there. You wouldn't have a positive chain of custody of the evidence anyway," said Sharon.

"Sharon, how do you know all of this?" asked Carl.

"Later," she answered, never taking her eyes off of Mike to check his reaction to the points she raised.

"I'm not sure how it's going to get done, Sharon, but it *will* get done." They all knew it would if the tone of Mike's voice was any indication.

"It's still kind of a leap to lay this all on Vernon Tripplete. I'll find out more about him and fill you in tomorrow night," said Maggie. "Sharon, I'll order food in, my treat, before we eat you out of business and home."

"I'm sorry, Maggie, but it will be a cold day in hell when someone eats carryout in my place. I don't see me going broke in the next week." Realizing she sounded a little harsh, Sharon added, "Besides, I have a plan."

"I think it's time we call it quits for tonight. We're all a little stressed and I have to go to work tomorrow," said Bernie.

Mike grabbed a sandwich for the road from a tray, gave Maggie a little hug, and followed Bernie out the door.

Sharon and Maggie cleared the tables. When they reached the kitchen, Maggie gently put a hand on Sharon's arm. "I meant no harm, dear."

"Oh, I know, Maggie. I guess I'm wearing a little thin. I don't know how you deal with it."

"I have a little secret, dear: I *don't* deal with it."

"Drive me home, Carl, not so fast over the bumps, if you please," said Meyer.

Carl stopped the chair at the usual corner of the building. The stars were in full array and not a cloud was to be seen.

"You miss your boat, I guess," Meyer said softly. "I used to watch you from my window. You were always the last one in every night, even when you were on crutches."

"I sometimes think Mom was right. I should have gassed up the boat and just drove away."

"At one time I would have agreed with her. But if we don't stop these people, they'll find another Alonzo King somewhere. People who are willing to kill once find it much easier the second and third time. You would have been Number Two, out of who knows how many. I can promise you one thing, son, they will be stopped soon, one way or another."

CHAPTER TWENTY-FOUR
Sense of Direction

Carl felt relieved to be doing something with his hands requiring no real concentration. Removing the red paint splashed onto Tad Anderson's boat went slowly. It was nearly ten-thirty before he took his first break. He had run out of the solvent Jeffords had given him to clean the footprint off his boat. It took a little more elbow grease to remove the paint from Anderson's schooner. The paint had only been on the boat for one day. Fortunately, it wasn't fully dried.

Chuck had just returned with six more cans of the cleaner when Sharon called Meyer, asking him to remind Carl it was nearly time to leave for Mount Zion.

"It's not Sunday, girl."

"We've been invited to a party, and we have to buy a birthday gift on the way. You tell him to get his butt in gear."

"You stay where you are. I'll send him over shortly."

Sharon hung up the phone and could hear the PA system at the boat yard come on with a squeal and a buzz. Meyer cleared his throat then announced, "Carl, Chuck, haul it in here now."

As they came in, Meyer asked, "Carl, what is this about a party? Why wasn't I told about this?"

"I'm sorry, Meyer, I didn't think it was important. We were invited before you grounded me."

Meyer scowled at the two men. "Chuck, go out and take the back seat out of the van again. Carl, clean yourself up, for God's sake. You're a mess. Get going. I have a call to make."

Forty minutes later, after the van had made a diversionary five-minute trip, it pulled up behind the diner. Chuck went in, brought Sharon out, and installed her onto the floor of the van, next to Carl.

"Everybody set back there?" asked Chuck as he climbed in and started the engine.

"Sorry about this bodyguard thing, but he's your Meyer, not mine. He insists I keep out of sight as much as possible," said Carl.

"It was a conspiracy between Maggie and Meyer, and she is your mother, not mine. Speaking of conspiracies, guess what your mother and I did today?"

"Is this a question I have a snowball's chance in hell of answering?"

"No, I guess not. Your mother forged me a set of really official-looking press credentials and I went to meet with one Vernon Tripplete."

"What in the hell?"

"Later! We're at the mall, gotta shop. Hurry up."

Carl had heard of power shopping, but never in his whole life had he believed it really existed. It seemed like in a matter of moments the circulation in his fingers was being cut off by the handles of the plastic bags he was lugging. He was certain he had done permanent damage to his neck muscles by contributing a nod of agreement and a smile whenever asked, "What do you think of this?"

Crossing the Centerline

Chuck met Carl and Sharon at the prescribed mall exit. They waited until he brought the van as close as possible to the door. Carl struggled to find a place to sit. The back of the van had taken on the appearance of the floor around a Christmas tree.

Sharon became very busy, taking the packages out of the bags to refluff the bows.

"Sharon, what makes you think Isaiah wants any of this stuff?"

"Don't be silly! Even if he doesn't, he'll enjoy getting it. It's the way people are. You ask someone what they would like for their birthday, they'll say, 'Oh nothing.' If you get them nothing, they'll never forgive you. You know what they say, it's the thought that counts."

Carl pondered in silence for a moment, then he remembered the conversation they had started when they got to the mall. "What in the world inspired you to visit Tripplete?"

"Well, Maggie and I couldn't sleep last night, so we sat up talking and…"

"Why do you listen to that woman? She's insane!"

"Carl Fletcher, what a way to talk about your mother."

"Did the thought occur to the two of you this man is perhaps a killer?"

"You know, we did consider it, but–no offense, Carl–he wants to kill *you*, not Maggie or me."

"What did you hope to accomplish there? What kind of credentials?"

"Press IDs. I interviewed him about the widening

of Highway 83. Really, I just wanted to get a look at him, size him up, you know. He doesn't look like a killer to me."

"What is a killer supposed to look like?"

"Not a mousy little man, balding, shaggy gray mustache. He had a very small office, thick with the smell of cigar smoke, and a suit looking like it might have fit him before he grew out of it."

"Did you ask him if he would consider giving up the hobby of wanting me dead?"

"Didn't come up. Maybe next time."

The van made a hard left, sending passengers and packages flying to the right wall of the van. Carl peeked out the back window to see the trees along the drive. A red jeep followed them for a short way, then turned sideways to block the drive.

"Take the drive down the left side of the church, Chuck."

"Don't think so, Carl. A rather large black man in a suit is blocking the road with his body."

"Don't run over him; he's the pastor."

"Gotcha."

Carl expected some reaction from Reverend Thompson when he saw them climb out of the back of the van, but there was none at all.

"Sorry about the entrance, Pastor, but Meyer insisted," said Carl as he rearranged his leg brace.

"Yes, I know. I talked to Jim earlier. I just didn't want the guest of honor to see you arrive this way."

"You know Meyer?" asked Sharon. A puzzled look on her face.

"Oh yes, for some time now. May I help you

with those packages? I believe you must be Chuck. I wanted you to know I suggested you join us for the party, but Jim would prefer you stay in the van near the corner of the church. I'm sure you understand. Refreshments will be brought to you shortly."

"I understand Pastor. Thank you, that's very kind of you," said Chuck.

"Kind is sort of my job around here. We'll see you later."

Carl and Sharon followed James Thompson past the church with the parcels in hand.

"You know, this wasn't necessary. I don't believe Isaiah is expecting gifts. He told me you promised to bring him a smile."

"That will make it even more special, a surprise and a smile. I don't ever remember seeing you at Meyer's shop."

"I'm sure it's true. I've never been there."

Sharon knew Meyer seldom left the shop, and her curiosity was boiling over. "But then…"

As they neared the patio, the reverend said, "We'll talk another time, okay." It wasn't a question.

There was bunting around the tables, a rainbow of balloons, and at least forty people gathered under the roof.

"There come my friends, there they come, and look at that pretty little gal in the yeller dress with flowers on it. I bet she knows that's my favorite color, yeller. What all them packages, gal? Don't say ya done bring them all for me."

"No, I brought you the smile you asked for. The packages are for me," Sharon said as she kissed the old man on the cheek. He kissed her hand in return.

"Let's all sit down now. We don't want all this food to go to waste in this heat. There is a chair saved for you, Sharon, at this table next to Isaiah," said Delphinia with a wink in her direction.

Sharon sat where she was expected to. Isaiah graciously introduced her to the woman on his left, his nurse Julia. "She kinda help me with some of the things I has trouble with, you know."

"Carl, why don't you and I take a little stroll while the others get their lunch? Delphinia, dear, please save a place for Carl and me," said the reverend.

When they were away from the patio, Carl said, "I know what you are going to ask. The answer is yes, we got information that indicates Alonzo was killed. You are welcome to it…with a proviso. I would like you to refrain from going to the authorities on this information until we exhaust all options of resolving this ourselves. We aren't certain how many or who all the parties might be that may have had a part in it."

"It appears Alonzo has waited over a year for the justice he would never have had without you. I'm sure he would have understood waiting a little longer."

Carl took an envelope from the pocket of his go-on-a-date suit coat. The envelope contained copies of everything Meyer had compiled. Carl handed it to Reverend Thompson.

"Thank you, son. I think it's time for lunch."

Lunch was an understatement. It was a feast, and

Carl enjoyed every bit of it. He asked for seconds on things he didn't even recognize. Sharon swapped recipes with several of the ladies, writing them on napkins with the reverend's pen. Carl had never seen her so happy.

The gift opening was supervised by Nurse Julia, who kept a scrupulous list of who gave what so thank-you notes would be timely and accurate. There were neckties both funny and beautiful, candies, and a watch from the reverend and Delphinia.

Sharon held back one of her packages, making sure Isaiah opened it last. It was a brass model of a locomotive with Alonzo's name engraved on the side where the number would normally be.

"I thought you might like to keep this in honor of Alonzo."

"I sure do like it, honey. It's a doozy, and heavy, too."

Isaiah was surprised and thrilled with all the attention. After the paper was cleared, coffee and a three-layer cake–each layer a different flavor–with buttercream frosting was served.

While the others filled their plates, Isaiah motioned Carl over. "Let's take a little walk, you, me, and your little gal there. You push."

When they were far enough from the group that they couldn't be overheard, Isaiah reached down to the hand wheels and stopped the chair. "Honey, the train you brung me, it's mighty pretty, and I like it just fine, but I feel funny about keeping it."

"Why is that?" "I thought you would like it."

"Oh I do, just fine, but you see, you and me got a

misunderstandin'. Lonzo didn't collect trains like that. He was fond of studying the other railroad, the North Star; you folks call it the Underground Railroad. That's why he loved his house so."

"You mean Alonzo's house was part of the Underground Railroad?" asked Carl.

"Why sure, I thought you knew when you gave me the pictures, with the tunnel doors showing and all."

Sharon was embarrassed, but recovered quickly. "I think you should keep the train, Isaiah. It's a fine train, and every time you and I look at it we can laugh at how silly I was."

"You wasn't silly, you just didn't know. You want to know, you go and ask the Missus. She knows all about the North Star."

"You mean Delphinia?" asked Carl.

"Yeah, she's the Missus. She knows. I think we best be moving on, 'fore the cake's all gone."

The party continued, with an impromptu concert by various members of the choir who sang solos and in groups. It was nearly five-thirty when Nurse Julia suggested perhaps it was time for Isaiah to get a little rest before the evening service. Everyone accepted the graceful hint. Carl asked Isaiah if it would be all right if he came back once in a while. Isaiah made it clear the price of admission was he had to bring the little gal in the yellow dress with him. This got him one more kiss on the cheek from the gal in the yellow dress.

Delphinia waited to walk Sharon and Carl to the van, to say her goodbyes.

Crossing the Centerline

"Delphinia, I know you're very busy here, but I was wondering if you could spare us a moment in the next day or so to chat about the Northern Star Railroad," asked Sharon.

"It was called the North Star Railroad, dear. I'm a little busy with services tonight. If you could come out tomorrow at, say, nine-thirty in the morning, I would be glad to tell you what I know. Of course, Carl is welcome too."

Chuck had the back door of the van open as Carl and Sharon reached it. The two weary travelers climbed in. The red jeep pulled aside to let them through. The two young men inside waved as they passed.

"This had to be the best party I never went to. I have enough food up here to feed an army. If you ever come back here for another non-party, can I not come again?" asked Chuck.

"Check with Meyer. We have to be back here again at nine-thirty tomorrow morning, and you are entirely welcome to not come with us," said Carl as the trees glided by.

Carl looked over at Sharon. As her eyelids closed, the recipe napkins slipped from her hand.

CHAPTER TWENTY-FIVE
Patience, Patience, Patience

The ride to Mount Zion the next morning was an improvement over the ride of the day before. Sharon drove Maggie's Taurus while Carl lay across the back seat. Chuck followed in the van. The red jeep parked across the drive after they passed, while they parked in the lot alongside the church.

Delphinia was tending the flowerbed girding a turnaround in front of the big wooden doors.

"Good morning to you all. I have coffee and some snacks, if you'd like to come this way."

The roof over the patio was welcome; the sun was already heating the calm day.

Carl placed a black briefcase next to his chair and set the legal pad he pulled out of it on the table, along with three new pencils.

"I see you and I have something in common, Carl: I also prefer to write with pencils. I believe it goes back to when I was a young girl. We didn't have a great deal. How I envied all the children whose families could afford new, long, bright pencils."

A soft look had come over her eyes, seeming almost like tears, as she stared down the long drive in front of them.

Delphinia twisted the handkerchief in her hands as if using it to pull herself back to the present. "I'm sorry, I'm sure you didn't come to hear about my childhood, you came about the railroad."

Crossing the Centerline

"If you don't mind, I know so little about this, I would like to take some notes," said Carl.

"Not at all. I must say it pleases me you show an interest in it. I doubt they teach much, if anything, about it in schools nowadays. It's a shame. It is as much a part of American history as it is Black history. Many abolitionists traveled to the South to teach the slaves what paths they should follow to freedom. Some of them were actually slaves themselves at one time. They had either bought their freedom or were freed by their masters.

"Many of the southern slaveholders felt if they kept the slaves unschooled generation after generation, their lack of literacy would hold them captive as well as chains could. Not being able to read and write, with no knowledge of geography, they wouldn't know what direction freedom was.

"The people who came to the south resorted to the most basic directions to educate the captives. The first was to show them the North Star. Even the smallest of children were taught how to find the Big Dipper. At that time, they all referred to it as the drinking gourd, like the type used in water buckets in the fields. The lip of the gourd in the sky would point the way to Polaris, the North Star.

"Of course, it wasn't possible for these simple people to remember the whole of these directions, so they made up songs with the directions coded into the lyrics for them to memorize.

"Along the way to the North, the abolitionists set up safe houses. The people who were on the run could hide at them during the daylight. There was food, rest, and directions to help them on their way to the next safe house.

"Our friend Alonzo found out the house over on Highway 83 was owned by a family, named Kraft, for generations, and it was called Kraft House. Prior to that, it was called North Star. Alonzo, when he retired, bought it from the Kraft estate and devoted himself to restoring it. Now, both it and he are gone.

"You know, when I was young, I would hear people say to those of us of color, 'Go back where you came from.' When I grew older, I realized my family has lived in this state longer than almost all of the white families who populate it now."

The soft almost tearful look reappeared in Delphinia's eyes. Carl could see it in Sharon's eyes, too. The reverend walked up to the table, sat down next to his wife, and gently put his hand over hers.

"Was Delphinia able to tell you what you wanted to know?" he asked as he handed her the handkerchief from his vest pocket.

"Even more," said Sharon, her voice cracking.

Another handkerchief appeared in the reverend's hand and Sharon pressed it to her eyes.

"I asked our congregation to pray for me last night. I told them I needed guidance, their prayers, and God's will to help me. I found Alonzo's will. There was nothing there that wasn't there before, but I saw it in a different way. Brother King left his home and all his worldly belongings to the church, with me as executor.

"Because the house burned along with everything in it, quite honestly I had more or less forgotten about it. Last night I realized that even though the house built by man's hand was destroyed, the land the Lord made was still there. I would like to do something with it, something that would have made Alonzo proud.

"I called the church's attorney this morning. He is filing the papers to proceed with probate today. I intend to have the congregation make suggestions about what we should do with the property. Delphinia and I would like to have you, our new friends, join us in the process."

"We really couldn't presume to tell you what to do with the land, but whatever you choose, we would be honored to help you do it," said Sharon.

"I must apologize for taking up so much of your morning," said Carl. "I can't thank you enough for all you have shared with us. Sharon, I think we better move on and let these people enjoy their day."

The Thompsons, hand in hand, walked Sharon and Carl to the Taurus and stood waving as they, tailed by Chuck in the van, disappeared down the long drive.

"Where would you like me to drive you for lunch, sir? The meter is running," Sharon said over her shoulder.

"What are we going to do about our escort?"

"Take him with us, of course. Whither we goeth, he goeth, according to the Book of Meyer. He is going to follow us anyway, whether we like it or not."

"Then I vote for The Sanctuary. I hear the food is

good and it seems appropriate somehow," said Carl.

As Sharon predicted, Chuck parked the van next to them. After some explaining on Sharon's part, he agreed. After all, it was almost noon. They all had to eat anyway; it may as well be here.

They were seated immediately. While they were looking over the menus, Carl saw Sharon's face go white, and he heard a man's voice behind him.

"Well, Miss Waters, fancy meeting you here. I hope you got all the information you needed yesterday. Don't get up, gentlemen. I don't believe we have met. I'm Vernon Tripplete. Miss Waters was kind enough to interview me for an article she is doing on road construction."

Sharon gasped for breath. "This is Chuck Howard and Carl Fletcher. We work together. Guys, Vernon Tripplete."

Greetings were exchanged. Tripplete said, "What a coincidence meeting you way out here. I was in Beloit pitching a job. We stopped here 'cause it was near the interstate. I'm sorry for interrupting; it was a pleasure to meet you gentlemen. Miss Waters, you all have a nice day."

"Yeah, small world. You have a nice day too, Mr. Tripplete," said Sharon.

Tripplete moved across the room to rejoin two other men in suits at their table. Sharon swallowed all the water in her glass in one gulp.

"When did you take up writing, Sharon?" asked Chuck.

Carl answered for her. "Yesterday. Hadn't you heard? You know, I bet she neglected to tell you we have a strong suspicion Mr. Tripplete is the person trying to permanently end my new career."

"I bet he followed us here from the church. Let's make a run for it," said Sharon, rising from her chair.

Chuck put his hand on her forearm, eased her back to her chair, and said, "No such thing. I don't know about this interview thing or why he's here now, but we don't run. You two order and eat your lunch. When you are done, come straight out the front door, get in your car, and drive directly to the boat yard, no matter if he and his group come out before or after you. Do you understand?"

Sharon and Carl nodded their understanding. Chuck got up, smiled at them both, as well as in the general direction of Vernon Tripplete, and walked out of the restaurant.

She tried to look at the menu, but Sharon's eyes kept wandering over to Tripplete's table. Carl finally convinced her there was no way Tripplete could have known where they were coming to eat, and he reminded Sharon that Tripplete was here ahead of them.

Sharon and Carl ordered sandwiches and did their best to eat them. Sharon finally gave up, asking for the check and a doggy bag from the waiter. Carl didn't debate who would pay the check.

They were two steps outside the door when the van pulled up. Chuck asked them if Tripplete or anyone from his party left their table or made a phone call. Sharon assured him neither of those things happened. Chuck told them it was okay for them to head back in the Taurus. "Take your time. You won't be followed by anyone but me." Looking at Carl, he said, "If you're a good boy, she might even let you sit up front."

Sharon didn't share Chuck's faith they wouldn't be followed. She spent the whole trip speeding up and then slowing down to make sure Chuck was still behind them. She drove the Taurus into the shop, parking next to Anderson's schooner. Meyer, sitting on a barstool, was removing paint from one side; Hank was replacing the lettering on the stern with gold leaf.

"Meyer, you'll never guess what happened," said Sharon.

"I don't have to guess. Chuck called me when it happened. How did you like riding up front like a big person, Carl? When Chuck called, I got hold of Mike. He ran a DMV check to get Tripplete's plate number. Chuck tells me he will be changing a tire before he leaves the Sanctuary."

"How did you know he wouldn't have someone else follow us?" asked Sharon.

"Because you told us. Think about it. When I talked to Mike, he asked if we could meet at the diner at four. He and Bernie have somewhere else to be later," said Meyer.

Sharon raised an eyebrow. "They have to be somewhere together?"

"I assume so, why?"

"Did he say where?"

"No, and I didn't ask."

"I wonder how we could find out?"

"Why would we?" asked Carl.

Sharon said under her breath, "Men are such idiots," as she headed for the diner.

Meyer and Carl trailed along. They came in the back door in time to see Nina, Maggie, and Sharon in a huddle behind the counter.

"Meyer just told me," said Sharon. "Do you suppose it's a date?"

Mike held the front door for Bernie, who was as dressed up as anyone had ever seen her.

"My, aren't we turned out? Where you headed?" said Nina. "Got a hot date or something?"

"Close, but not exactly. We can only stay for a minute."

Sharon and Carl explained what they learned at Mount Zion and their accidental meeting with their prime suspect, leaving out the flat tire part.

"Mike, did you have any luck with the blood stains?" asked Maggie.

"Not yet, but we should have some good news after tonight."

Carl reached for his ringing cell phone. He walked outside to hear better.

"Carl, Charlie Thompson. I'm afraid the plans we spoke of this morning for Alonzo's land have hit a dead end. Our attorney just called. He informed me we have no right to the land. It seems that shortly after the remains of the house were condemned and torn down, the land was seized by the county under the right of eminent domain. Our attorney is trying to get copies of the paperwork. We probably won't see them until tomorrow at the earliest. From what he has learned, he assumes they took it as part of the highway expansion."

"I was just out there, Reverend. That section of the road is finished except for some grass seeding. The house, or what's left of it, is a good two hundred feet from the road. I don't understand."

"I'll call you in the morning, after the lawyer calls, to let you know what he has to say."

"Thanks for the call, Reverend. I'll talk to you then."

Mike and Bernie had already left when Carl got back into the diner. He asked, "Anybody know anything about eminent domain?"

"Sure. When the government wants your land, they are supposed give you full market value for it, but you really have no choice, you have to sell for the good of the community. That's the plus side of living on a boat, Carl; when they condemn it, you can just move it. I suppose someday they'll claim my place so they can tear it down to build a timeshare or something there," said Meyer.

"You mean they can take your land and sell it to someone else to use, even if it's not for a road?" asked Carl.

"That's what the law was written for. Nowadays the 'community good' can mean damn near anything," said Meyer. "There are always lawsuits filed against it, some even get to the Supreme Court, but they usually don't change anything. It's tough to fight City Hall."

"Mom, could you nose around with the computer and see what is happening locally like this? Meyer, I'm headed down to my boat, want to come along?"

CHAPTER TWENTY-SIX
If Dreams Came True

When they reached the star-watching corner, Meyer grabbed the hand wheels of the chair and spun it to face Carl. "What's bothering you, son?"

"What isn't? All of our lives have been thrown into the air. Every morning for the last week, if I look out the windows to the bay, there has been a man walking the pier with a dog. This morning, when I looked, the two of them were climbing off of my boat."

"Oh, my fault. He's a friend of Mike's. Works security at the airport; the dog is a sniffer. Mike asked him to drop by every day on his way to work, just in case. It lets Chuck and Hank get a little extra shut-eye. I didn't think you would mind, but either Mike or I should have told you."

"It's okay. The bad thing was how scared I got. We should have hidden the boat again after the police were done with it."

"My experience has been that it's hard to set a trap without bait. Miss the water, do you? You know there is an old saying, sailors and boats rot at the dock. Maybe we can fix that."

Meyer spun the chair, rolled past the shop, toward the pier. "I could see this coming. There is only so long people like you and I can stay away from the water, Carl."

The repaired runabout was already in the water.

The waves lapping at her sides sounded like she chuckled in anticipation. Carl helped Meyer down into the leather seat behind the wheel, untied the mooring lines, and walked the boat to the end of the pier, pointing the bow out toward the bay. One quick shove as he jumped down into the back got them started. They idled away from the slip, letting the engine warm up.

"She's got a full tank, son. I hate driving around in circles like some damn weekender. Where should we go?"

"Out onto the lake, up to Port Washington. We should be able to get there in time for a fish sandwich at Larry's."

"So it shall be."

They veered to avoid a speeding small boat coming through the cut in the breakwater.

"That looked like that nitwit Teddy. His old man finds out he has his boat out again, he might skin him alive," said Meyer, shaking his head. "You know, I don't believe the boy will ever learn a thing in his whole lifetime."

When they arrived at Port Washington, Meyer turned the boat to enter the mouth of the river which fed into the harbor. A few minutes later, Carl tied them up at the fuel dock of Carlson's Marina.

John Carlson came out of the small building on the dock just as Carl was lifting the chair out of the runabout.

"And what's all this, laddie, fall out of that penthouse of yours?" said Johnny in a booming brogue that echoed throughout the harbor.

Crossing the Centerline

"Ah, Johnny, times are hard, ain't they now? This is what happens when you run with the wrong crowd. We came for a sandwich and a brew. It would be an honor to have you as our guest."

"I may have a minute to spare, if it means the opportunity to see your wallet open. It could be a once-in-a-lifetime event."

One sandwich, several beers, and a ton of stories later, Meyer was ready to call it quits.

"Carl, I'm afraid you'll have to become a chauffeur. I don't trust me to get us home. Let's go, boy, or it'll be daylight before we get there."

Meyer slumped over as much as the cast would allow, as he dozed all the way back to the boat shed. The sun was indeed just coming up as they arrived. As Carl helped him into the chair, Meyer said, "It's off to work, boy. Let's go."

"Work? What about sleep?"

"We have the rest of our lives to sleep. Now we work."

As they rounded the corner of the shop, Meyer nearly wheeled into Sharon's shins.

"I have reported your boat stolen and you two kidnapped. I better go call Mike and cancel the search. You know, Carl, I am somewhat used to this guy, but I expected better from you. You, your mother, and I are expected at Mount Zion in one and a half hours. I suppose you can come too, Meyer. It might be an opportunity for you to repent."

Sharon turned on her heel and double-timed it back to the diner. Carl and Meyer watched the door slam behind her. They turned to each other, and all

Carl could say was, "HUGE."

Meyer and Carl used the extra time after showering and changing to practice on the crutches Hank had picked up from Dr. Blackman. Meyer bowed to Carl's experience in adjusting them. They were so uncomfortable Meyer was certain they were set for a gnome and said so.

They all got into the van, with Sharon driving. Chuck followed at a respectful distance in the Taurus.

"Wait till you see the driveway, Mom. It's one of the prettiest places I've ever seen."

"That's my boy; a driveway is his favorite place in the world."

It wasn't long before they made the turn into Mount Zion. Under her breath, Maggie whispered to Sharon, "He's right, this is gorgeous."

"I heard that. I think an apology is in order."

Sharon turned in her seat. "Don't hold your breath back there, boat boy. Every time we come here, that red jeep is sitting there, and when we go by they turn it to block the road. It's the reverend's way of making sure we're not followed, I guess. I think it's sweet, don't you, Carl?"

Meyer whispered to Carl, "I guess she hasn't seen the sniper on the roof of the church."

Carl's head swiveled toward Meyer. "What sniper?"

"What did you say, Carl?"

"Nothing, Mom, nothing."

The reverend and Delphinia were sitting on the patio with a tall balding young man in a gray three-piece suit that screamed *I'm a lawyer and proud of it*.

"Reverend Thompson, Delphinia, this is my mother, Margaret. I understand you and this gentleman already know each other."

Delphinia brought a chair around for Meyer and kissed him on the cheek. "Jimmy, we finally got you out here. I wish it were under better circumstances."

As Carl was pondering anyone calling Meyer 'Jimmy', the reverend stood, shook Meyer's hand, and said, "It's a pleasure and an honor, sir."

"Charles, it is great to see you again. Thank you for the consideration you have shown for my friends."

"We'd like to believe they are our friends also."

Maggie, Sharon, and Carl began to feel as if they were the only ones not in on a joke.

The reverend introduced Rasheed Jackson, the church's attorney.

"A pleasure to meet all of you. Sharon, how nice to see you again. It must be what, five years?"

"At least, Rasheed. I'm pleased you represent Mount Zion. It's their good fortune to have you."

"We look upon Mr. Jackson as one of the many gifts the Lord has granted us," said Delphinia.

"I'm sorry to bring you out here on such short notice, but I think it would be best if you hear what Rasheed has discovered in person. There isn't a great deal more at this point than what I said on the phone, Carl. I did want you to meet Rasheed; you may feel free to contact him at any time about this matter. I have told him about our shared predicament. He is willing to offer his services in any capacity he can," said Reverend Thompson with a nod to the attorney.

"I'm assuming Sharon has shared the process of eminent domain with you, so we can move right through the sequence of events I have discovered. The petition for condemnation was filed the same day Mr. King's home burned down. I believe we are all in agreement; the house catching fire was not by chance or an accident. It is my thought, in light of that fact, there was, and may still be a public official involved in these activities. We should not only be gathering information to fight the case of eminent domain but also be building a criminal case for the attorney general to prosecute.

"I have prepared a request for injunctive relief. It is being filed by my assistant this morning. We are asking for a stay of any activity regarding this property until we are allowed a hearing to appeal the execution of eminent domain. I understand you have gathered information about some activities surrounding this affair. Would you be willing to share what you might feel is helpful with me?"

It was clear to everyone at the table that he addressed the question to Sharon, who answered, "The reverend told me you might ask for the information we had gathered. We have a copy of the record Meyer has prepared. I do have to caution you, Rasheed, some of it can be testified to, but some of it may be opinion on our part. Be careful what you use."

"Point well taken. Perhaps after we gain a little more information, some of what appears subjective will change to fact on its own, or at least will appear that way," said Rasheed.

Crossing the Centerline

As Sharon slid a file folder over the table in the direction of the attorney, Maggie and Carl stared at her as if seeing her for the first time. Meyer's expression never changed during the whole discussion. He glanced from Sharon to Rasheed to the pastor and his wife.

Meyer fixed on the reverend. "Charles, have you made this young man aware of the situation he is entering into here, the possible risk involved?"

"I realize you don't know who I am, sir, but if it wasn't for you, I probably wouldn't be here at all. I know what is going on; if you'll let me, I would like to help stop it. The U.S. Supreme Court handed down a five–four decision this morning; it said it was none of the federal court's business whether a local or state government exercised the right to claim private property for private development. That means the only way we can save Mr. King's land for the church is to have the government, or whomever they granted or sold it to, give it back by abandoning the condemnation, or we need to prove the land was taken improperly. It would be best to be able to show we tried to bargain in good faith with whomever holds the rights to the land in case we do go to court later. It will show we attempted to resolve the issue without litigation," said Rasheed.

"Rasheed, when you see the information in that file, I'm sure you'll agree almost certainly Vernon Tripplete or his paving company is or will soon be the owners of that land," said Sharon.

"As I understand it, a man who works for him is the person you suspect of trying to eliminate Carl here. I would suggest Carl not take part in the negotiations."

The attorney's dry delivery brought a smile to everyone's face but Delphinia's. "I think I should go see Mr. Tripplete as the representative of the church. Sharon, since you've already seen him, could you figure out a way he might see me?"

Sharon put out her hand in Carl's direction. He knew full well what she wanted. When she raised one eyebrow and snapped her fingers he relented and surrendered his cell phone.

"Good morning, this is Sharon Waters from the *Daily*. We met the other day, yes. I wondered if I might have a word with Vernon for just a moment? Thank you. Mr. Tripplete, well, it's good to speak to you too. Sir, something interesting has come up in my research for your story. I wonder if you could spare me a moment to discuss it. No, it shouldn't take long. Thank you, it's very kind of you. Sharon grinned as she snapped the phone shut and returned it.

"He can spare us a few minutes, if we get there in a half hour. He has another meeting in Beloit after lunch."

Meyer knew better than to argue with Sharon at this point and said, "I would prefer Chuck drive you, if that's okay?"

"It's perfect. Tripplete thinks Chuck works with me, so he can come right in with us."

"Charles, what do you think?" asked Meyer.

"I would like to follow along."

"Sharon, would you like to take my pen, in case

you want to take notes?" offered Rasheed.

"How much recording time does it do, son?" asked Meyer, much to Rasheed's surprise.

"How did you know?"

"A lack of subtlety on your part, son. If it were just a pen you would have laid it down on the table instead of pointing it at people like you were interviewing them for the six o'clock news. It's new, isn't it?" asked the reverend.

Rasheed hung his head. As he packed his briefcase, he didn't reply.

Meyer stood on his crutches. "If you'll pardon me, I'd like a word with Chuck before he leaves. Would you care to join me, Reverend?"

CHAPTER TWENTY-SEVEN
Just When You Thought You Knew

Sharon drove to Tripplete Paving Contractors. Delphinia showed Chuck how to use the camera she had loaned him to give credibility to his presence at the meeting.

Marla the receptionist was not in her usual chair. Instead a bottle-blonde with troweled-on makeup was in her place. "Can I help you folks?"

"Hello. I'm Sharon Waters, for Mr. Tripplete."

The blonde informed them Mr. Tripplete was really quite busy; she was his wife Betty and wondered if she could be of help.

"I spoke to him just a short time ago and he said if we hurried over he would make time for us."

"I don't know why he always does that. I'll go check with him," said Betty Tripplete as she placed the mirror she had been staring into on Marla's desk. She returned shortly with Vernon Tripplete trailing behind her.

"Come in, Sharon, please. Who are your friends? Oh, I met this gentleman at the Sanctuary yesterday. I don't believe I've had the pleasure, ma'am, I'm Vernon Tripplete."

"I'm Delphinia Thompson, sir. It's my pleasure, I'm sure."

"Now that's a name I recognize. You would be the pastor of Mount Zion's wife, am I correct?"

"That's true."

"Then I must apologize. We have met before, although it was some time ago. I paved that long driveway at your church; I was a foreman at Carmichael Contracting at the time. I'm sure you don't remember me, though. No offense intended, but it was a long time ago, I'm afraid."

"Not so long ago. I remember now, you used to wear a gold helmet with a bird painted on it."

"Yes, I painted a peacock on my hard hat. My first wife Doris said when I made foreman it made her proud as a peacock. It was sort of a joke between us. There are a lot of days I wish I was still just the foreman or somewhere painting birds."

Tripplete slumped into the chair behind his desk, suddenly looking a great deal older. "What can I do for you people?"

"I would like a picture to go with my story and a comment from you about the U.S. Supreme Court's latest decision about eminent domain, particularly how it's used by local governments to help developers. Gifting them with someone else's property, so they can do what they wish with it."

"I didn't know the Supreme Court got involved in anything like that. To answer your question, I think it's a horrible thing. Now, I know our company has paved over property the state or county has taken in by the process, but, I tell you, it makes me sick. I'm just glad we don't get involved with any of that part of the business. By the time we're out there pushing dirt around, all of that stuff has been handled by whoever hires us."

"Are you telling me you haven't ever taken part

in a condemnation process or taken possession of land that has gone through the process?"

"Of course not, Sharon. The only land I own is this lot where the business is and the one my house is on. For the record, I still owe money on both of them. What are you getting at? Did someone tell you I got land condemned for my own benefit? I'd like to know who said it. I'll sue the hell out of them. I have enough trouble keeping track of what I have now. I don't need any more problems."

Delphinia, who had been quietly trying to let Chuck know he would have to remove the lens cap from the camera if he was even going to pretend to take pictures, leaped in to try to calm Mr. Tripplete down. "I'm certain, Vernon, there has been some kind of misunderstanding. It happens all the time in the newspaper business, you know. That's why Sharon has to constantly check and recheck, just like she is doing with you right now. I know both of you are pleased she was able to clear this up before she wrote her feature about you, aren't you, Sharon?"

"Yes…yes, I'm sorry if I upset you, Vernon, but check and recheck, that's what I do. Neither you nor I would want something in print if it wasn't the whole truth, would we?"

Delphinia rose from her chair. "Sharon, I think it's time we got on to the flower show. Chuck has to get his pictures before they all start to wilt. Thank you so much for your time, Mr. Tripplete. It was so nice to see you again, after all this time."

There was nothing else for Chuck and Sharon to do. They followed Delphinia's lead, said their goodbyes, and filed out of the office. Sharon was frothing by the time she got to the car. She tossed the keys to Chuck and climbed into the back seat. "What was that all about, letting him off the hook with you apologizing to him?"

"It seemed like the thing to do. After all, we were close to directly accusing him of fraud–and worse– when it was obvious we were wrong."

"Wrong? How do you figure, wrong? This guy is trying to get Carl and who knows who else killed."

"No, dear, I'm sure he isn't. We went there wanting to believe he was, but it simply isn't true, as much as we want it to be. He certainly wouldn't have lied about claiming land when he would know how easy it would be for you to prove otherwise."

"What do you mean, it isn't true? Who else could it be?"

"I don't know, child, but of one thing I am certain: Vernon Tripplete doesn't have a clue about any of this business. I have spent the greater part of my life listening to people proclaim their innocence, saying how everyone else is wrong but them. I've developed, shall we say, an instinct for separating the wheat from the chaff. I'm sure Mr. Tripplete isn't golden wheat. I also know in my heart he isn't the chaff we thought he was."

"Why not?"

"Because anyone who is in love has no time for evil."

"So he loves his wife, so what?"

"Not his current wife. Dear, he still loves the wife he lost. The question may be, why not this one?"

"I'm sorry, Delphinia, but I have a hard time believing you can get all that in the short time we spent there."

"As a pastor's wife, I have the opportunity to study how people act and why. You learn to stand in the background while everyone talks to him and ignores you. That distance often allows you objectivity, affording you the opportunity to learn. You see, the problems from person to person are very often the same; only the faces change. When you see the same thing over and over, you recognize it early. We were wrong. Mr. Tripplete is not what we wanted him to be."

"You know, I think it would be a good idea for you and the pastor to come to dinner at my place tonight–you know, the diner, nothing fancy–and you can explain to the others why we are off base and how."

"I'm sure Charles would be delighted and so would I. We seldom get away. It's so kind of you to offer," Delphinia said, ignoring the fact the invitation was really a challenge.

Chuck and Sharon had assumed the rest of their group would be gone when they returned to Mount Zion. Instead, Meyer had borrowed a spare wheelchair. He sat beside Isaiah and the others on the patio near the residence.

It was obvious stories were flying; the newcomers could hear laughter all the way out in the parking area.

"Well, here comes my little gal now. I could tell you was up to something, got them all worried about you. Are you folks all right? I could tell you was on their minds."

"We're all fine, Isaiah. Might I say your new tie is a winner," said Sharon as she bent to give him the kiss on the cheek he now expected.

"Charles, we have been invited for dinner at Sharon's restaurant tonight at six. I hope you don't mind, I accepted for both of us. Do you know the way there?"

"Yes, Delphinia. Thank you, Sharon, how kind of you."

Meyer rose out of the chair and Carl handed him the crutches. It was everyone's cue; Meyer felt they had worn out their welcome. "It's that time, boy. You still owe me a day's work."

As Carl helped Meyer into the van, Maggie and Sharon left in the Taurus.

"Maggie, do you believe some people have the ability to read other people in the first few moments they meet?"

"Yeah, in some cases I think they can. Not necessarily all the time with everyone, but sometimes yes, yes, I definitely do. Don't you?"

"I guess I'd have to say no. It's just not logical."

"Then I must be totally screwed up. I liked you the minute I met you, and I was right. You are very much worth liking. I suppose if you don't believe you could even like someone on first sight, then there isn't love at first sight either."

Sharon glanced at the van in the rearview mirror; Chuck was at the wheel. "I guess you're right. There are some people you know are what they appear to be and are worth knowing. You want to help me cook for tonight?"

"I think I'll do everyone a favor. I'll do what I do best: run the dishwasher. I'll watch and chat, though, how's that?"

"Even better. Maggie, you haven't heard from Mike or Bernie today, have you?"

"You'd be the first to know if I had, kid. Count on it."

Chuck pulled the van into the shop. As he helped Meyer out, he commented that Hank was nowhere to be seen.

"He's running a small errand for me," said Meyer. "Would you go down to the dock to see if he finished your project? Call me on the walkie-talkie if it's done."

"You got it, boss."

When Carl reappeared with his work clothes in his hands, Meyer asked him to push him over to *One Fine Day*.

"Why? Is there something wrong with her?"

"I don't know. You tell me when we get there."

Expecting the worst, Carl nearly dumped Meyer out of the chair when they hit the joint between land and pier. As they neared the boat, Carl could see the stern was covered with a tarp.

"Well, pull it off, Chuck," said Meyer. "Or do I have to climb out of here and do it myself?"

"Guess you will, boss, 'cause I ain't going to."

Meyer rolled up to the tarp and gave it a tug. The stern of the boat had been repainted and lettered with gold leaf.

ONE FINE DAY
BAY HARBOUR WI.
CAPTAIN CARL FLETCHER

"Holy cow, Meyer, I can't afford this! I mean, I'll pay you as soon as I can, bet on it, but–"

"Do you like it, Carl?"

"Who wouldn't, but–"

"Good, then we're even. Be sure to thank the boys. They did it. I just furnished some stuff."

CHAPTER TWENTY-EIGHT
The People You Meet

Maggie and Sharon were driving the regular cook crazy just by being in his kitchen. Sharon was sure no matter what she made, it wouldn't be good enough, and the diner would never be clean enough.

Shirley and Nina had twice washed the tables in the back room where the group usually met. The floor had gotten double duty also. When Sharon asked if they thought she should replace the drapes, they went back to the dining room shaking their heads. Sharon heard one of them say, "All this just for the reverend and his wife?"

Carl spent the afternoon attacking the vandal's handiwork on Anderson's sloop. He was happy to do it, figuring he now owed Meyer a great deal more than that. Anderson showed up and accused him of taking his time so Meyer could charge him more. Carl found himself in sympathy with Teddy: the more some people had, the worse they behaved.

He finished the cleaning so Hank could work his magic repainting the hull. Carl sat on an overturned pail washing the red paint residue from his hands. He suddenly remembered looking though Sharon's telescope and seeing someone else do the same thing.

Hank returned from his errand by the time Carl had cleaned up. He dropped a box on Meyer's desk. "Boss, you want Chuck and me to paint up Anderson's tub so we can roll it out in the morning?"

"I know it's a lot to ask, Hank, but I would really appreciate it."

"No problem, boss. I don't like that mouthy bastard coming around here either." As Chuck and Hank used the stairs to get down to the shop, Hank stopped to comment on Carl's white shirt as he entered the great room.

"Gonna try that date/non-date thing again, hey rookie? By the way, nice job on the sloop. You may catch on yet."

"Thanks for the lettering, guys. It was a great surprise."

They threw him a wave, never looking back.

Meyer opened the box. Carl could see it held about a dozen pairs of handcuffs.

"What in the hell are you doing with those? You going to start your own police department?"

"I told you the other night this thing has gone on long enough. I said it would soon be over one way or another, remember?"

"Yeah, I remember. Listen, I would be the last guy on earth to tell you what to do, let alone what not to do, but Bernie and Mike have a lot at stake here. I sure hope you aren't planning anything that would land them in hot water."

"That's very noble of you, son, considering you are the one who could end up dead if this keeps dragging on. I thought you knew me well enough to know I wouldn't do anything that would harm those two. I've grown fond of Bernie and can almost tolerate Mike," Meyer said with a grin.

Meyer decided to crutch his way to the diner. As

he got used to them, he appreciated the improved mobility they gave him over the wheelchair. As he said, it was time he got on the move.

Nina whistled as Carl came through the door. "I didn't know you had dress-up-like-a-big-boy clothes there, junior. Going to church, are we?"

Carl could see the red flush creep into her face as she noticed the reverend coming through the door behind him.

"No, Nina, I thought I would bring the church to Carl tonight. How are you, Nina? It's been a while. Still can't convert you to a Baptist, huh?" said Reverend Thompson.

Delphinia took both of the old woman's hands and kissed her cheek. "You look great, Nina. Stop by for tea next Wednesday. We have so much to catch up on," said Delphinia.

Carl asked the pastor and his wife if there was anyone in town they didn't know.

"You live long enough, you meet them all, son," said the big man.

Maggie and Sharon were still fussing with tablecloths when the other four came into the back room. Sharon welcomed the newcomers, and invited them to sit where they wished. She brought them all iced tea, then she and Maggie joined them.

They agreed to wait for Bernie and Mike before they started dinner. While the other four engaged in polite conversation, Carl asked Sharon for a moment alone. "Sharon, did you keep all of the pictures you took the other day when you first showed me the telescope?"

"I think they're in the tray under the tripod, why?"

"Would you bring them down for me? I'd rather not tackle the stairs. Mike may need them in a while."

Carl rejoined the others in the back room just as Bernie and Mike came into the diner. It was obvious Bernie had been crying.

Maggie immediately put an arm around Bernie's shoulders and with a glare in Mike's direction asked if she was all right. Maggie automatically believed somehow Bernie's tears were Mike's fault.

"I'm okay. It just hasn't been a very good day. In fact, it was a horrible day," said Bernie.

"Come along upstairs, dear. We'll splash some water on your face and get whatever this is straightened out."

Delphinia rose from her chair and went with them, as if there was an unspoken invitation.

"What is this all about?" asked Meyer.

"She got through all her entrance exams for the academy last week, was accepted, then went for her physical today. They rejected her for height. She honestly thought she was a half-inch taller than she is. I really feel sorry for her. She's wanted this for a long time."

The reverend looked at Mike. "Would she have made a good officer, even if she's a half inch too short?"

"Second to Carl here, I can't think of anyone who I would rather have as a partner."

"Are you sure you feel that way because of her ability or because you like her as a person?"

"I'll tell you, Reverend, you have to like your partner or you should get a new one. She and I have only seen each other away from here or the job once. That was last night and it was really business."

Reverend Thompson looked in Meyer's direction and saw the slightest nod. "I wouldn't tell her or get her hopes up, but perhaps all is not lost. There may be a slight chance I could help with this."

Carl had no understanding of how, but he felt the reverend and Meyer would be able to help, if anyone could. "Let it go, Mike. These things do have a way of working out."

The ladies returned from upstairs. Bernie seemed to have regained her composure. They all served themselves from the buffet Sharon and Maggie had prepared. While they ate, they observed Maggie's rule of no business at the table.

When coffee was served with cherry pie and cinnamon ice cream, Sharon realized no one had introduced Charles and Delphinia to Mike and Bernie. She rectified the oversight, and also told them of the meeting with Rasheed and his offer to help.

Sharon then explained their second meeting with Vernon Tripplete, omitting Chuck's struggle with the lens cap. She did, however, ask Delphinia to explain why she thought Tripplete was a highly unlikely suspect and why perhaps they were on the wrong track in pursuing him. They wanted to believe the pastor's wife, but they were running out of suspects.

After they had discussed Delphinia's theory, Mike cleared his throat, his usual technique for getting everyone's attention. "Bernie and I spent most of the last two days trying to find a way to connect either Wiley Tucker or Symons, the guy who tried to do away with Carl, with what we all agree was the murder of Alonzo King. After we had little success on our own, we got together for dinner last night with Rick Collins, Will Wise, and Ron Snyder, the medical examiner. We asked them what we would have to do to connect these two to the crime, even if it wasn't admissible evidence. We were hoping if we could charge them and get them to talk before they realized the blood samples we have couldn't be used in court, perhaps they would give up whoever hired them. Ron Snyder agreed to get us DNA testing through his office of samples we would supply, if we could get a warrant to justify getting the samples.

"Wise told us he didn't think we needed to get samples from Tucker. He was sure there was some of his blood on the bottle he cut Collins with at Ziggy's. Collins couldn't remember it at all, but Wise was certain an EMT had bandaged Tucker's hand and arm before the back-up unit took him downtown. He assured us he had bagged the bottle as an exhibit and dropped it off at the evidence room that night.

"Super-clerk Bernie had a friend of hers in Evidence check it out. Sure enough, the bottle is still there. I guess when Reece got the case shelved, he forgot about the evidence still being around.

"Snyder says he needs a court order to open the case, so we have to show a judge that we have just cause for the case to be reopened as murder, not an accident. At that point, we have to take it to my boss."

"A court order we can get with a phone call," said Delphinia. "That's what little brothers are for, isn't it, the occasional court order as restitution for all the times he tagged after me as a kid?"

Meyer's eyes had widened. "Little Dickey is a judge? Well, I'll be."

Delphinia laughed at Meyer's reaction. "I thought you knew, Jimmy. Criminal Court One. Money well spent, I'd say."

"I know my reputation as a cook or baker isn't the greatest," said Maggie. "But here is the icing on your cake, Mike."

"Go ahead, Maggie, make my night."

"After we met with the church's lawyer—one smart fella, that young man—he called me and gave me tips on finding out who claimed the land at Highway 83 and Council. It is an LLC named Wiltrip. It turns out the officers in that corporation are Wiley Tucker, James Reece, and not Vernon Tripplete, but Betty Tripplete, Vernon's wife. The corporation filed for ownership less than a week after their friend got elected to state office. Reece and a buddy of his sit on a committee which approves property transfers and state loans to improve blighted areas. Wiltrip had already applied for a zoning change to commercial, from agricultural, under Alonzo King's name to be sure they could get the zoning change before they bothered to kill him."

The pastor handed his wife a handkerchief and asked, "Delphinia, would you please call your brother and ask him to come here at once? Perhaps you had better invite Rasheed also."

CHAPTER TWENTY-NINE
All Good Things

Everyone helped clear the table and got all the dishes into the kitchen, where Maggie took charge of the dishwasher. While they waited for the new invitees to arrive, they sipped coffee. Carl invited Mike over to the shop to see what he had worked on for the past few days.

When they reached the lights of the shop, Carl showed Mike the photos taken through Sharon's telescope of Teddy washing red paint from his hands and the pictures Hank took of Anderson's schooner slathered with red paint.

Mike slowly shook his head. "This is when you really learn to hate this job, when you have to accuse someone you know. Crap."

"I was thinking about that. We really don't have any hard evidence yet, and maybe never will. So if you talked to Teddy and his parents and they promise to get Teddy some counseling.... Well, what's done is done. The insurance companies aren't going to get their money back, and what good is Teddy in jail, anyway?"

"They have a new phrase for this downtown now. They call it community continuity. First-timers serve a kind of parole, they don't get a record, and if they behave and don't repeat, they never get a record."

"If they do repeat?"

"Their ass turns to grass and I get to be the lawnmower. I'll take it to the sheriff in the morning to get his approval. I think I'll ask Meyer to give me a hand with Teddy and his folks. I understand he knows them pretty well. Thanks for the help, Carl. This could have got ugly if some boater with a gun caught him at night in the marina."

The two of them checked out Hank's paint job. As they headed back to the diner, Carl mentioned Meyer's handcuffs purchase.

"I don't have an answer for that. If it all works out maybe I won't need one. You know what they say, ninety-nine percent of what we worry about never happens. Let's hope they are right."

Delphinia's brother, the judge, hadn't arrived at the diner yet when they got back. Sharon and Rasheed were reviewing the latest information added to Meyer's notes. They agreed Mike's plan to reopen the death of Alonzo King was good, but didn't know if the judge would approve it. As Mike and Carl entered the room, they all were debating whether they should let Mike know about their doubts.

Sharon called a halt to the discussion to remind everyone present that if the blood testing fell through, they were back to square one.

"Mike, Bernie, Rasheed, I would appreciate it if you would leave the room for a moment," said Meyer.

When they were gone, Meyer took Sharon's hand in his and said, "I know you may look on this as vigilante justice but, as I told Carl earlier, it is time this comes to an end. It's our intention to do this the proper way if possible. If for some reason it can't begin to be resolved in the next twenty-four hours, Hank, Chuck, and I intend to let the people involved know that if they take any more action, they do it at great personal risk, and we intend to make them believe it. Sometimes, Sharon, violence has to be discouraged with violence. We can't tolerate these people putting our friends or possibly you at risk."

Just then Judge Wilson arrived and Mike showed him in. Delphinia made the introductions then asked her brother to sit down and listen. Rasheed explained the history of the situation. Like the good lawyer he was, Rasheed used Meyer's notes as an aid to emphasize those points he felt would sway the judge to issue the warrants they wanted.

When Rasheed was finished, Judge Wilson asked for a few moments alone with his sister and brother-in-law. The three of them strolled through the parking lot together. It was obvious the judge was looking for a polite way to start the conversation. Finally, his patience broke.

"What in the hell are you two thinking? Do you realize how close all of you are to committing several infractions of the law, not to mention what this could do to your reputations and standing in the community?"

"A great deal of what you just heard in there was brought to light within the last hour, Jimmy. All of the pieces just came together; that is why we called you right away. Tell me honestly, do you believe this investigation should proceed?"

"Of course it should, Del, but that isn't the point.

What do you think the sheriff is going to say about all the evidence you people haven't shared with his department? I know at least one of the people in that diner is a deputy. He won't be for long if his boss thinks he has been withholding evidence in a homicide."

"Jimmy, you heard how everything progressed. There was never any intention to avoid the system. There was no case, as such, until tonight," said Charles. "I don't think even Rasheed has considered what might happen when this comes to light. I don't believe the deputy in question is so stupid he hasn't considered it. All he was trying to do was build a case to take to his superiors and at the same time protect his ex-partner and friends. Now all they need is a little help. You and I can provide the help and you know it."

"Charles, are you sure you should risk all you have done and become for this? What if we fail?" said the judge in one last effort to sway two determined people.

The reverend put his arm around the waist of his wife and told his brother in-law, "This is our life. We are here to serve. This is just another opportunity to do so."

The judge shook his head in resignation. "What do you want me to do?"

"Jimmy, Meyer and his friends need the warrants you can give them. Charles and I are going to see the sheriff in the morning to explain how these people have helped us look into the death of one of our dearest fiends. It would be very nice if you would consider joining us."

"You had to throw Meyer into the mix. You know, Del, for a preacher's wife, sometimes you can be a real pain in the ass."

"I know, Jimmy, and sometimes I actually enjoy it. Let's go make a list of what Sharon and Rasheed want."

Charles nodded at Rasheed as the three family members returned to the meeting room. Rasheed handed the judge a slip of paper. "If at all possible, your Honor, I would like to pick these up in the morning, if it's all right, sir."

"Give me a number where I can reach you. I understand I have a rather early meeting to attend," said the judge, giving his sister a look little brothers save for older sisters. "Del, Charles, good evening. It was a pleasure meeting all of you. Meyer, I believe I will be seeing you in the morning."

As soon as Judge Wilson was out of sight, Mike dialed the medical examiner's number. "Ron? Mike. We'll have the warrants in the morning. You did? Great! Okay, I'll send him down right now, great."

Mike dialed another number. "Rick, Mike. Where are you? Ron needs a blood sample from you; yeah, right now, he's at his office. It'll put you one step closer to cuffing Tucker, that's why. Right now. Thanks. See you in the morning."

It was agreed there was little to be done until they had the lab results. There was a flurry of phone number exchanges and 'I'll call you ifs' as everyone departed.

* * *

Meyer pounded on Carl's door. "Come on, get ready, we have to be there in half an hour."

"Be where?"

"We're going to visit your old boss."

"You aren't going to tell him about this, are you? Mike could get canned."

"That's precisely why we *are* going to tell him, so Mike doesn't lose his job. Come on, let's go."

The Thompsons and Judge Wilson were waiting for Meyer and Carl at the door of the sheriff's office while the two of them did their best to negotiate the steps. When the receptionist showed them in, Meyer indicated to Carl he should wait in the lobby.

After better than an hour, the sheriff came out of his office with the others trailing behind. "Carl, how are you? Your friends here explained how the charter business has been set back temporarily. It seems they are doing their best to get it back on track. You give me a call as soon as you're ready. I want to be your first paying customer."

The judge excused himself to meet with Rasheed. As the others approached the van, Carl's cell phone rang. "Carl here. Hi Mike, any news from the lab yet? No kidding, when? Well, that worked out better than I thought. Okay, see you there in five minutes. Carl hung up and dropped the cell phone into his pocket.

"Mike just told me his boss called him to inform him a group of citizens dropped by to thank him for allowing one of his officers to work on his own time to resolve a miscarriage of justice. He was so convinced of the outcome of Mike's investigation he told him to assemble an arrest unit. Isn't that astounding?"

"It's marvelous how the sheriff appreciates the young man's service to the community," said Delphinia. "I'm positive if the guilty parties are brought to justice, as they should be, the members of the Mount Zion community will remember what the sheriff and his men did this fall at election time."

"Mike also said he would like all of us, if you'll pardon the expression, to get our butts over to the diner."

A number of unmarked and squad cars lined the rear of the diner parking lot. All of the drivers of the cars were gathered in the meeting room where Mike was chairing the gathering.

"I'd like you all to meet the district commander of the state patrol, Martin Vance. He will be acting as liaison with the attorney general's office. His men will handle the arrest of the senator when we signal them to do so."

A groan went up from the assembly.

"Come on, you guys, you know we don't have jurisdiction in Madison. Besides, the state cops with those cowboy hats make for great photos in the papers. Rick Collins will be arresting Wiley Tucker on accessory to murder. Miller and the two O'Conners will arrest the other two, who were at Fern Hill, on weapons charges. Those charges probably will not get us a conviction unless they confess and cut a deal. Chris O'Connor has been tracking these guys on his own time. We can be almost certain they'll show up at Ziggy's near four o'clock. We want to be in the building when they arrive. Unless you hear from me, meet back here at three."

The officers left.

"She'll be here any minute now. Play it straight until Nina brings in the cake," said Mike.

Seconds later, Bernie came through the door and soon Nina followed with a cake lettered edge to edge with 'Congratulations Cadet Bernie, You are now a COP.'

No matter how many times Mike tried to explain how the selection board had changed their decision, Bernie couldn't understand. She was still puzzling it over when Mike received a call from Ron Snyder.

"Thanks, Ron, all I can say is thanks," said Mike, and he closed his cell phone. "We have them, everybody. I know there is a long way to go, but at four we take them," said Mike.

"Sharon, if you wouldn't mind, I'd like to stay here until this is over," said Delphinia.

"Of course. What say I whip up a little lunch? Mike, will your crew be back here to eat?"

"No. I think I'll have them meet at Ziggy's instead."

The afternoon dragged by. At about two-thirty, Mike declared it was time for him to go. Shortly after he left, Meyer suggested Carl and Charles join him down at the boat yard.

"I'd really like to be there for this," said Sharon.

"I think Charles, Carl, and Meyer will do a fine job of representing us at Ziggy's. We have something else we should take care of right away," said

Delphinia.

"Ziggy's?"

"I've know Meyer and Charles for a long time, dear. When they left here, there was no doubt in my mind where they were going. Now, who'll drive us to see Mr. Tripplete?"

"I suppose you're right, we better get there right away. It would be a shame if he found out from the news or some stranger called," said Sharon.

Bernie stared at the other women in disbelief. "Find out what? Tell him what?"

"We think someone should let him know Mike will be arresting his wife within the hour. I imagine it will be quite a shock for him," said Maggie.

Marla, the receptionist for Tripplete Paving, asked politely if Mr. Tripplete was expecting them. Sharon explained it was most important they see him immediately. Marla disappeared into his office. In a moment Vernon Tripplete followed her out to the lobby.

"Good afternoon, ladies. I didn't expect to see you so soon. Do we have more check and recheck to do?"

"You might say that, sir. If we could have a moment in private?" said Sharon.

"Of course, Sharon. Please come inside. The day is almost done. Can I get you some refreshment, a beverage of any kind?"

"I don't think so, sir. May I introduce my friends? This is Bernadette Wilson, and this is Maggie Fletcher, and of course you know Delphinia.

Maggie is going to tell you a story that starts a little over eighteen months ago. Then I'll bring you up to date with what's happening today. Maggie?"

Mike wasn't totally surprised with what he saw when he entered Ziggy's. Seated at a table in the farthest corner were five men: two in coveralls, one with crutches, another with a brace on his right leg, and a large black man who seemed to have misplaced his suit coat and clerical collar. He did his best to ignore them as they anted up and dealt the next hand.

Shortly after Mike took a stool, Miller and O'Connor took seats at the opposite side of the oval-shaped bar.

The cell phone in Mike's pocket started to vibrate. It was Chris O'Connor, signaling that the work crew was leaving the job site. Mike started a conversation with the bartender about how hot it had been recently. All the players understood they had less than ten minutes before their quarry arrived.

No one expected the size of the crew, including Mike. There were fourteen, not counting Wiley and two of the men who tried to gain entry into Maggie's apartment at Fern Hill.

Realizing he and his group were badly outnumbered, Mike improvised. He walked over to the card players' table and tapped Carl on the shoulder while he hit the speed dial button on his cell phone. Carl slowly stood up and positioned himself to the left of Wiley Tucker as Rick Collins walked through the front door, then to Mike's side. Mike and Collins freed the snaps on their holsters.

* * *

"I know it's difficult for you to believe, sir, but we do have copies of paperwork here proving your wife and her partners, Wiley Tucker and James Reece, were obtaining properties by condemnation along Highway 83. It also appears they were leveraging your paving firm to finance a shopping mall at Council and 83. That was the location of the home of the man they had killed. He was murdered because he had applied for the house and land to be designated a historical landmark. If he wasn't removed before it happened, they would never have been able to build the strip mall they planned," said Sharon.

"You do believe us, don't you Mr. Tripplete–Vernon–you aren't really surprised, are you?" asked Delphinia.

The little man sadly shook his head and sank even deeper into his chair, wishing he could disappear.

"Is your wife here? They will probably be coming for her soon," Delphinia said gently. "They are out at Ziggy's now, arresting Tucker and two of his friends, who came to Maggie's house with guns looking for her son, Carl. We can only assume that was going to be a second attempt on his life, because they believed he suspected Mr. Tucker's involvement in the murder."

Tripplete looked into Maggie's eyes and whispered, "I'm so sorry for this. I didn't know. I should have, but I didn't know."

"Where is she, Vernon?"

Allan E. Ansorge

* * *

Mike, Rick Collins, and Carl stepped up to the table of Wiley Tucker and his friends.

"Good afternoon, Mr. Tucker. Let me introduce myself and my friends. Of course you already know Detective Collins. This is Fletcher; I don't believe you have met face-to-face before. I'm Detective Mike McCaffery. We are here to arrest the three of you for attempted murder, and Wiley Tucker, you are under arrest for murder, arson, and attempted murder."

One of Tucker's friends got as far as the front door. He was met by Chris O'Connor, who had already drawn his gun. His partner from Fern Hill didn't see the crutch come out in front of his feet as he attempted to run into the kitchen. He was quickly gathered up by two men in coveralls and deposited in a chair for his own safety.

Mark Miller and John O'Connor stood on the bar, holding their badges overhead and their guns drawn to convince the rest of the crowd to behave.

Wiley Tucker made a dash for the rear exit, but bounced off a large black man and fell to the floor. Before Tucker could recover the small handgun he dropped, Rick Collins had rolled him onto his stomach and was cuffing him.

Vernon Tripplete drove to the salon where his wife was having her hair done to pick her up.

When he reached Council, he drove out to Highway 83 and turned right at the intersection with the burned-out house.

"Where are you going, Vernon?"

"Just down the road a bit."

Betty Tripplete didn't notice the four women in the car following them.

Mike McCaffery had just finished his call to Commander Nelson when his cell phone rang. "Mike? It's Bernie. We brought you a present. It's in the Lincoln pulling into the driveway now."

"I'm telling you, Vernon, I'm not going into a dump like Ziggy's, you take me home *now*."

"You won't have to go in, dear." Vernon Tripplete pushed the child safety switch that unlocked the car doors.

Mike opened the passenger side door, reached in with a set of handcuffs, and said, "Mrs. Betty Tripplete, you have the right to remain silent…"

EPILOGUE

"Sharon here."

"Good morning."

"Hi Carl, where are you? Where have you been, fishing?"

"I haven't had a charter in weeks. I spend most of my time delivering boats to wherever rich people want to sit on them to watch the sunset. When they are tired of that spot I move them to another place."

"Have you heard from Mike or Bernie at all?"

"Mike called to say Bernie graduated from the Academy and starts patrol duty in a month. Mike got a promotion, you know."

"No kidding! What is he doing?"

"They put him in charge of reviewing cold cases."

"Your mom stopped by yesterday. She picked up Meyer to drive him to therapy. She is moving out of Fern Hill. I guess it has gotten too quiet for her."

"So she says. What are you doing?"

"I'm thinking about going into catering and…"

"No, I mean right now. What are you doing right now?"

"Nothing, I guess."

"How about we take the boat up to Terry Andre Park for a picnic?"

"That sounds almost like a date."

"Oh yes, it is *definitely* a date."

"Huge."

Crossing the Centerline

* * *

Like the two small kids they would still like to be, they sat at the end of the pier, side by side. Their feet dangling in the water, their hands occasionally bumping into one another on the pier, they squinted out over waves that looked like glittering gold.

"You ever been to Key West?"

"No. Never been anywhere really."

"Every sunset is like this. During the day, the water is so blue you just can't believe it."

"Someday…"

"There is a bed and breakfast one block off Duval Street that has a dog that surfs in their pool."

"You're kidding, right?"

"Nope. Her name is Daphne. She takes a running jump from the side of the pool onto an air mattress and glides right across."

"Huh. I'd love to see that."

"Friday. We'll go Friday."

He deliberately placed his hand on hers.

"Huge."

About the Author

I was born in Wisconsin and currently split my time between there and Florida. I find it a necessity to come back North occasionally where sanity is the norm, and people at least pretend to obey traffic laws.

I grew up in a small town where you didn't misbehave because everyone within ten miles would know about it in five minutes. It was a town where everyone under voting age knew anyone's mother could smack them if they chose to get out of line.

A four room schoolhouse didn't offer a large number of literary options but Crazy Quilt (a horse who slept in a bed covered with, you guessed it a QUILT!) and The Boxcar Children (orphan children raising themselves while they live in a…. you fill in the blank!) introduced the non-academic mind to story telling.

One might think not seeing a real library until I was a freshman in high school might have stunted my appetite for reading. In my case what had been withheld became a treasure. Picture if you will a teenage boy who actually read the articles in playboy. The joy of the written word stayed with me through my career in business and brought me to authorship later in life. As I say "late is much better than never."

Printed in the United States
221245BV00001B/1/P